A TASTE OF
HONEY

RAVRY SLOAN

A Taste of Honey
Copyright © 2012 by Ravry Sloan
Ravry Sloan, LLC
ISBN: 978-0-578-16411-3
First Edition

New Testimony:

Abundant life comes from knowing God and fulfilling His purposes for your life. It has taken me 8 long years since I published my first novel, Beyond the Blues, but that did not mean I was not being obedient to God's calling and direction. Since that time I have grown so much spiritually, as a woman and as a writer.

First, I began to accept who I am, where I come from and what I am made of, but then I had to figure out what I was supposed to do with all of this. I had to find a way to let go of the things I did in my past, what others did to me and things I cannot change by simply forgiving. Once I found it in my heart to forgive; God took over and began showering me with His many, many blessings.

I am so excited about my life and all that He has to offer! I wake up daily with the anticipation of God fulfilling all of my heart's desires by giving me new ideas, placing the right people on the pathway to my journey and allowing my dreams to manifest. God has taught me that it is a choice to decide to live in peace and with joy in my heart and on January 1, 2011 I made the decision to live in the moment and to live my life out loud!

I am confident that God did not reveal my purpose in my life for me to fail or fall so giving up on my dreams is never an option. I committed to my dreams by asking God to teach me and show me what I must do to be prepared for my prayers to be answered and He has done just that! I give all honor and glory to God as I welcome you to the birth of my new dream...*A TASTE OF HONEY!*

I have identified with what brings me peace and joy, and not only do I try to get it done; I eagerly wait for my desires to be fulfilled. Don't just dream of hope, prosperity and success, believe in them and make them happen!

Hugs & Kisses,

Ravry Sloan

Dedicated to the memories of:

Rev. and Mrs. Lee and Tammie Jones, my loving grand-parents:
65 years of a dedicated marriage…
a real example of what true love, commitment, faith and strength
should look like.
Thank you for showing me how to love and live!

Shandra "SISTER" Williams:
One of my best friends
who taught me how to accept life and love people unconditionally!
I love you & miss you dearly!!

Dedicated to:

My aunt, Kathy Stevens:
Thank you for always guiding me, supporting me and loving me.
You have always made yourself available to me when I was weak
and lost in darkness.
You've shown me by directing me towards the light, which is my
power source!
I am so PROUD of you for getting your
degree…CONGRATULATIONS!!

Heartfelt Thank You's:

To my children; my heartbeats, my reasons for living... I am so very PROUD of the both of you:

Terry Dawson, set the bar high, stay focused and keep reaching for your dreams.

Raven Sloan, create the path you desire to travel and be fearless on your journey.

To my loving and always supportive parents...You have always given me room to grow and supported me the entire journey:
Calvin and Eleanor Stevens, my examples of family, faith, fun and fellowship.

To my brothers...Thank you for loving me unconditionally and for supporting me, even when I was wandering around in darkness:
David Stevens and Calvin Stevens, Jr.

Along with a host of family and friends!

Special Thank You's:

To my neighbors and friends for always looking out for me whenever I was at my emptiest:
Patricia "Nobella" Henderson, The Chef and Joel Powell, The Baker!

Dedicated Reading Team:

Cheryl Ellison, Evangelyn Tutt-Caver, Johnnetta Morris, Ranada Owens, Tracye Osby, Dr. Alix Pierre and George James IV.

Book Contributors:

Artist: Reginal Gillumo
Graphic Designer: Mario Robinson
Photographer: Dion Stanford
Interior Book Design: Junnita Jackson

Editors: Cheryl Ellison and Ranada Owens

My Dedicated Support System:
Thanks for always believing in me and encouraging me to FINISH
THE BOOKs:
Cheryl Ellison, Vangi Tutt-Caver, Kirby Arnold, Tanya Baugh-
Johnson, Johnnetta Morris, Guyla Darnell-White, Tanya Morgan,
Quandrell Claybrooks, LaKeba Wellons, Isaac Lee, III, Hank
Stewart, Galen Williams, Lucretia "Cree" Strawder & Family,
Tyra Peterson, Ranada Owens, Joel & Nobella Powell, Nichole
Patrick-Stevens, Margo Roberts, Latressa Nalls, Sonya Mason-
Corley, Dwan Bosman, Hudson On Bass, Gary Harris, Martin
Blockson, Antoine Knight, DeWayne McMillan, Ed Stroud, Allen
Smith, Teddy White, Dunkin N. York, Saderia Williams, Princess
Sugar Baby, Bettie Daniel, Billy Odum, my Spelman College
Family, James Simms & Simms Books Publishing, Simon & Hedy
Meyer, Katerina Mia & Kat's Café Staff.

HONEY

HONEY.... Marinating on your tongue

Dripping off your lips

(Sweet Words)

Bees can be the comparison of men

Like men bees search for that sweetness

That only HONEY can bring

(Desire)

They come across many exotic flowers hoping to find the ultimate HONEY.

Paying no attention to the delicate form, beautiful colors, roots planted firmly,

Stature, strength, etc, etc,

(Overlooked, Delusions of grandeur)

Only to find that the HONEY is still the same, just the flower is different

(The search continues…)

dramarotica (n.) /drah-*muh*-**rot**-i-*kuh*/

- A progression of events dealing with strong emotional conflicts; surrounded by chaos and confusion dealing with the art of sexual love.

- Combining highly expressive stories dealing with everyday social issues associated with intimacy and romance in relationships.

CHAPTER 1
A Good Thing No More

TROY WILKINS...

     As I stand in the elevator admiring myself in the mirrors on the interior doors I think, I'm not a bad looking brother. I'm the color of your darkest thoughts and desires--good health, nice dresser, successful, beautiful daughter, fine ass wife-- why can't that be enough for happiness? I wonder what I would do if I lost all of that?

     I look a little bit harder at myself, then thought, there is no way possible I can get caught, I'm just too good and I've been doing this far too long! I got this! I took one last look in the mirror as the elevator doors opened and off I strut to this sweet piece of ass that I know wants to please me and only me.

     "Hey, Poppi!" she screams as she runs and give me a great big hug and kiss upon entering into my corner seventh floor loft.

1

A Taste Of Honey   Ravry Sloan

"Hey, how's my sexy little lover?" I inquire while she immediately starts tantalizing my hardness, which was already standing at a full attention. Just the thought of how good Honey's sex is and after looking at her provocative ass in that outfit I knew I wanted her right then, right now. Her ass is playing peek-a-boo from under the bottom of the shorts, her hardened nipples in that cheap wife-beater staring me right in the face, and the scent of her sweet smelling fragrance lingering in the air.

"I'm good now that you're here. I missed you, Poppi, what took you so long?" she says mimicking a toddler by poking out her lip and crossing her arms rocking her body from side to side. "I thought you forgot about me today."

"What matters is that I'm here now, right?" I ask really not wanting her questioning my whereabouts. "You know better, my business is my business."

"I know, Poppi, I know. By the way, is today finally the day that you're going to tell me you left your wife?"

"What did I tell you?" I express very hardheartedly.

"I know, I know but you said you would probably be gone by the time of your daughters' birthday? Well isn't her birthday coming up?"

"I'm tired of you asking me about my business. Don't ask me about my wife anymore and never ever mention my daughter, again! My life and family are my personal business and you don't have any business asking me about either one, so as soon as you get that through your hard ass head we can move forward."

"Okay, Poppi, relax it's just that you've just been telling me that we are going to be together as a real couple and I'm just getting tired of waiting. It's been two years now and that date you said is coming up, I'm just anxious to be your woman and your woman alone. How long will I have you today anyway?" she asks grabbing my hands signaling for me to run them along her tight little body.

"I'll let you know," I answer as I noticed a big black bruise on her hip and left arm making my sex lay back down. Something

2

about it just didn't feel right. "What happened to you?" I ask showing somewhat of concern.

"Oh, that's nothing, Poppi. A customer got a little physical with me the other night. It's no big deal, I'm fine," she explains trying to throw me off the subject.

"I can't tell you what type of job you should be doing, but how long do you plan on being a *stripper*? You know all you have to do is get your GED and I can hook you up somewhere making good ass money with great benefits."

"Thanks, but no thanks. Like I told you before that is not my scene, Poppi. I can't be working no nine to five taking bullshit from *the man* and jealous ass women. I won't be able to dress how I want to dress and I'll always be on somebody's damn clock. No thank you, I don't see how you do it?" she says as she grabs me around my neck to kiss me gently in my ear.

"I don't…remember, I own my own business, remember? I am the boss, I do what I want to do, when I want to do it, where I want to do it," I say as we both laugh. "Enough of that, why don't you come on over here and take care of your Big Poppi the way I know you can," I state looking down at the huge bulge in my pants.

"Now that's what I'm talking about, Poppi," she states excitedly as she kneels down in front of me and unbuckles my pants looking up at me with a hungry look in her eyes. She slowly unzips my pants making them fall down around my ankles. She gently strokes my hardness up and down, teasing him with a slow kiss forcing me to let out moans of expected pleasure.

"You like that?" she asks looking seductively in my eyes pushing me back to fall on the sofa.

"Ooh, yeah, Baby," is all I could muster up to say while I relax and enjoy watching all of me slide in her slippery mouth. She feasts on my dick like it was her last meal. She slowly allows my dick so slide out of her mouth, looking deeply in my eyes, and quickly straddles over me. She slides my entire hardness deep inside of her wet, hot pussy.

I sat up to put those well-formed nipples in my mouth as she grabs my crown making me feel like I am her king. Our bodies embrace in a rhythmic motion. The intensity was high, our skin burn with pure ecstasy as she leans back making her firm nipples stand straight up in the air. I hold the small of her back in my hands as I guide my hardness deeper within her space causing her body to tremble, releasing her juices and screams of pleasure.

I didn't stop, extending her ecstasy until my turn to burst within. I cup my hands around her shoulders, forcing me to dig deeper and harder and faster and deeper and harder and faster, until an eruption with great intensity and magnitude cause us to simultaneous release love cries, paralyzing our bodies releasing of our orgasms. Still in a lover's embrace, she collapses into my chest as I fall back on the sofa, trying to gain control of our breaths.

"Oh my, Poppi, that's exactly what I needed," she testifies through uncontrolled pants.

"You ain't never lied, Honey, thank you," I express as I tap her on her ass cheek signaling for her to get up.

"I have some good news, Baby," she excitedly exclaims, but before revealing the news a knock tapped on the door.

"Are you expecting somebody?" I ask kind of baffled who could be coming to my loft on an early Sunday morning unannounced.

"Mr. Wilkins, its Morris from the leasing office."

"I'll get it," Honey said kind of abruptly running toward the door with her shorts still in her hands.

"No!" I command, "I got it. Besides who pays the damn bills around here, you or me? And he did ask for me didn't he? Now, move and go sit your ass down somewhere."

"Hi there, Mr. Wilkins, since the manager saw you come into the building he asked me to come by and get you to sign the disturbance violation that occurred here two nights ago."

"A disturbance violation, what violation?" I ask as I looked angrily at Honey with distrust in my eyes.

"Oh, Poppi, let me explain. I…"

"Shut the hell up, Honey, I'll deal with you later!" I calmly shout cutting her off and ending any chance for her to lie.

"Two nights ago, Mr. Wilkins, the same young man that has been escorted off of the premises on two other occasions, returned trying to call on Ms. Sinclair," explains Morris nervously.

"A young man huh?" I state as I review the words in my head and giving Honey the look that could have slit her throat.

"Yes sir, a young man. Each time he was escorted off of the premises was because of complaints from your neighbors about the loud music and talking from their drunken guests. And the smell of marijuana smoke in the hallway."

"Okay, tell me something, Morris, is this young man a frequent visitor to Ms. Sinclair?" I ask trying to get as many facts before I beat the shit out of her little ass.

"Poppi, wait please let me explain! You see..." she says trying to convince me she did nothing wrong.

"Save it and shut the hell up!" I unsympathetically say so I wouldn't back hand her in front of old Morris.

"We hate to disturb you with this, Mr. Wilkins, but following the lease and tenant agreement, we have no choice. I am also obligated to remind you of the three violation rule where as you can be asked to terminate your lease immediately upon the third violation and since this is the second violation we felt compelled to remind you again of this clause in your lease."

"Second? I never received the first. When was this?"

"Oh, it was about a month ago. We have the signed violation on file in the office, Sir, if you'd like to see it. As a matter of fact, you can read over this violation carefully, then sign it and bring it down with you to the leasing office before the end of business. I'll make sure to pull your file so you can review the first signed violation," explains Morris.

"Thank you, Morris, I will without question look over this violation and I will certainly be inquiring further about the other violation."

5

"Okay, Mr. Wilkins. You have a nice day and again I'm sorry for the unfortunate incident," he says looking a little relieved for me not shooting the messenger.

I didn't say a word to Honey I just stare at her for several minutes trying to read her expression.

"What the f*ck, Honey! What in the hell were you thinking? Did you think I really wasn't going to find out about some nigga being up in my shit? Tell me!" I shout as I reach for her neck making both of us land on the honey colored hardwood floors.

"Troy!" she tries to scream though my tight grip around her neck and in between trying to grasp for air.

"You know I could kill your dumb ass right now if I wanted to don't you? Don't you?" I yell but not really looking for any answer.

Then I thought about it, realizing that bitches like this are everywhere and she is not even worth all of this hassle. Panting like I just ran a marathon, I got up and kick her as I step over her to get my keys and cell phone.

"Troy, please...please, don't leave!" she pleads repeatedly. "What I want to tell you is that I think I'm pregnant, Troy!" she yelps which seems like an effort to try and get me to leave her alone.

"Bitch please! What game are you trying to play here? Do you really think I am supposed to believe you're pregnant and I'm the father after finding out about *this* shit? Have you lost your damn mind, Honey? I just really don't understand you, Honey, why? Why would you pull a ghetto move like this? That's what's wrong with all of you young *girls*, just too damn immature to recognize a good thing when you have it. You just messed up a great thing, Honey, a real great thing by being too damn childish."

"Troy, I don't know...I just don't know. I'm so sorry, Poppi, I messed up and I messed up big time. Please believe me when I say that it was not my fault," she says trying to cover up with more excuses and lies.

6

"Not your fault? Do I look like a damn fool to you or do you think you can out smart me. I tell you what, you and that baby better be out of my shit by tonight. Do you hear me? Last night was the *last* night that you will ever give my pillow some head and my bed some ass!" I express in a very pissed off manner.

"Come on, Poppi, don't do me like that. What am I supposed to do? I have nowhere else to go," she declares sobbing hysterically.

"That's your problem not mine. You better ask that nigga you were up here laying up with. As a matter of fact, give me my damn keys to my Escalade and the keys to my shit! You don't have to worry about the credit cards you can consider them already cancelled. And you better not take shit out of here that is mine or else I will make you regret ever playing these hoe' games with me. Matter of fact, I'll get Morris to help escort your ass out my place, put you in a taxi and send your ass far away from here!"

"Poppi, I'm so sorry." she whines as I walk toward the door.

Yodra and I might have our problems, I thought, but she would never disrespect me like that. Hell…I should have been home with my family all of these years in the first place. I keep trying to find what's missing at home in these damn streets and I'm getting sick and tired of the headaches. At least I know Yodra loves me and that's more than I can say about the rest of these females out here trying to get my money but not fulfilling their positions in the game.

****

Honey is my exotic little mistress who makes me feel like a man is supposed to feel and listens and fulfills all of my wants and needs. She's my short, sassy, Dominican/black mixed, sexy little freak. She will do any and everything to please and satisfy all of my sexual desires, no matter how unusual. She seems to make it all about me each and every time.

A Taste Of Honey   Ravry Sloan

The biggest thing that bothers me about Honey is her lack of ambition and goals. We've been doing our thing for about two years now and about six months ago I put her up in a loft so I can have a taste of that ass anytime I want to but I don't think she really wants much out of life. All she ever seems to talk about is being a famous video stripper. She's been *attempting* to get her GED for a while now, about a year, but really how long does it take?

Now, Yodra is the total opposite of Honey when it comes to pleasing me sexually. Unlike Honey, Yodra chooses her days to make me feel like I want to feel. Yodra is boring to me in the bedroom and is not spontaneous and exciting at all! She makes me feel so disconnected and so rejected like she's uninterested in me at times. I need some action, not always love making, bill paying and expectations. I'm especially sick of the expectation to please her and sometimes I just don't feel like pleasing but I just want to be pleased. Every now and then I just want some plain old selfish sex and that's why Honey is in the picture in the first place.

I don't have the balls to break Yodra's heart and I didn't work hard all of this time to give her half of my hard earned money, either. Hell, now that I think about it if it weren't for me she wouldn't have shit! I know we both started these magazine companies together but I'm the one who really put in all of the hard work, especially after she had Ivory-Jade. I ran both magazines and I think I deserve the bigger piece of the pie.

I'm the man who made Yodra into what she is today and that should be thanks enough, but an educated black woman always wants something from nothing. I'll be damned if I pay her to be with another man, that is not going to happen, over my dead body...over my dead body.

CHAPTER 2
What Next?

HONEY SINCLAIR...

Not knowing exactly where to go and what to do, I found myself sliding back to my old lovers' condo for help. I know we ended things kind of abruptly a couple of years ago, but we've always remained good friends. A concerned hand is just what I needed and has always been extended to me in my many, many times of need and loneliness.

"Who is it?" the voice on the other end of the intercom spoke.

"It's me, Honey."

"Oh hey, You, come on up its open."

I hate always coming here every time I hit rock bottom, but what else am I supposed to do? I have no one else to turn to and nowhere else to go right now. My family does not support my decision to be a stripper so going home is definitely not an option. At least CeeCee has a place to stay and is very financially secure.

"Hey, Honey," CeeCee speaks embracing me tightly as we met me at the door.

"Hey, CeeCee, it's so good seeing you. Hmm, you smell so good," is all I could say trying to sound unmoved by how I was truly feeling. "What is that you have on?" I ask before recognizing that I was actually trying to hide something.

"Just a little something, something I got as a gift. So what do I owe this surprise visit? What's happening?"

"I'm sorry…" was all I can say after a surge of tears escape from my eyes.

"Honey, what's wrong? Who did this to you?" CeeCee asks after spotting the fresh bruises on my neck.

"You know me, always making stupid decisions. I'm so not in the mood for a lecture so please, no judgments, not right now. I've had something I've wanted to share with you but I was afraid of what you would think about me."

"Really? Is that how you really think about me?" CeeCee asks looking a slight bit perplexed.

"Sometimes, but either way her it goes. I've been messing around with a married man since our break-up and this time I think I really messed things up. I do, however, think he's making more of this situation than it really is.

I'm so sorry to always have to come to you when I'm lost and lonely again, but CeeCee, I need you right now. He took the Escalade back and threw me out of the loft. I'm scared! I've used all of my money to put my things in storage and I'm too embarrassed to even go back to the club. I've been living in an extended stay hotel all week trying to figure out my next move."

"Honey, why didn't you just come to me sooner? I'll be the last person to judge you and I understand more than you know. You know you can stay here as long as you like, but I do have to tell you something," CeeCee expresses sounding a hesitant.

"Oh, CeeCee, did I come at a bad time? I can find somewhere else to go if I have to," I state concerned that I may be interrupting something as I head back to the front door.

"Wait, why don't you just stop talking so much and come back sit down and listen. That's always been part of your problem, you talk too much sometimes. What I am trying to say is I am working on a relationship so I hope you can handle that? I had to fill the empty void you left in my life and in my heart and at some point I had to realize I couldn't keep sitting back waiting for you to come back to me."

I felt a lump well up in my throat, but I tried to smile like I was being a happy and supportive friend. "That's good, CeeCee. You deserve it. You're such a good, caring person; you should have the love you want in return. I'm sorry I wasn't ready to give it to you then, but you know you'll always have a special place in my heart and my life. Is this special person here? Can I meet her?" I ask trying to sound excited.

"Well it's kind of sort of complicated right now and I'm trying to deal with some issues on my own, so just be patient and just allow me to tell you about it when the time is right. Hopefully, you will meet her soon.

"She's really sweet and I promise you'll like her. She's good to me and makes me feel really good as a person. She really spoils me and we laugh all of the time. She thinks about me as much as I think about her and that feels good.

"Like that fragrance you asked about when you first came in, it's called Rain Shadows, a rare fragrance she brought over from Africa just for me. She really took a lot of risks because she wanted to make me happy. She loves me that much and she has not only shown me that, but has also shown me there is no cost, nor consequence that she wouldn't risk for our love and for me."

"Well it definitely sounds like she'll put her life on the line for you and your love, and look, out of all of that you smell good, too!" I respond as we both laugh.

"So, it's the little things like this that lets me know how much she cares. She gives me rare and exotic things just because she wants me to have the finer things that no one else has. Can you believe she actually smuggled this into this country just because it reminded her of me and our love?"

"That's awesome. I can hear the love in your voice as you talk about her," I comment feeling even lower because I want to be loved and talked about like that.

"You know I never stopped loving you right? I'm not sure you understand how much I was in love with you, but I at least understood that you just weren't ready to be a part in my life and I can't do anything but respect that," CeeCee reveals as we embrace for a few minutes, feeling each other's heart beats and our body's trembling from nervousness about our conversations.

"Thank you, CeeCee, I needed to hear, know and believe that I actually meant something to somebody," I state pulling back to reveal what's going on in my life. "I have, well I guess it would be good news to share with you, too."

"Before you do, let's get you settled in then you can fill me in. You can unpack and freshen up if you'd like and I can finish cooking my dinner. I made chicken Alfredo fettuccini with a Caesar salad. Have you eaten yet?"

"No, I'm good," I reply actually feeling a little numb knowing that I can be so easily replaced and life *can* move on without me, imagine that?

"Are you sure? You know what, I'm not going to take *no* for an answer, we will sit on the balcony and eat dinner and have some wine like the good old days and talk. Besides, it looks like you haven't had a good meal in a long time. Come on, get going and I'll meet you on the balcony in a few. Okay? Then, I promise we'll finish talking."

"Okay, okay, you've talked me into it. Thank you, CeeCee, for just simply caring about me. I've always been able to depend on you. You've never turn your back on me and I really appreciate you for that."

"No problem, Honey, as long as I'm alive, you'll always have a home here with me."

"Thanks, Love," I answer as I went into the room to change clothes.

I can only depend on CeeCee for a minute so what's next, I thought? Troy is going to regret the day he dumped me like a bag of trash. Maybe I was wrong to have Lenox come over, but he didn't have to react like that. He has a woman and family at home and I'm just supposed to sit back and *wait* for him? That shit is just crazy!

I need to come up with a plan, and quick. I'm broke, but that's only temporary. I have no car, nowhere to stay and I maybe down but I'm not out...yet. How in the hell am I going to be able to explain to everybody that I am just another broke ass stripper with the dreams of a man saving me? This is so f'cked up. That damn Troy, he'll regret f'cking with me. How embarrassing is this shit?

"How about we have a nice glass of Chardonnay to go with dinner?" CeeCee asks pouring the wine.

"I really shouldn't but I'm so stressed right now, who cares. This maybe just what the doctor ordered."

"So tell me what's going on in your life, Mami?"

"It's funny you just called me that because that's the news I need to tell you. CeeCee, guess what? I'm pregnant!" I blurt out and burst into tears.

"Pregnant? Oh Honey, don't cry," while wrapping comforting arms around me. "How far along are you? Is this married guy the father?"

I release a big sigh because I really wasn't ready to answer all of these questions right now but I couldn't keep this a secret for much longer, so I answer honesty. "Yes, he is the father and I'm late. I've taken two home pregnancy tests and one said positive and the other said negative."

"Have you been to a doctor yet to confirm?"

"No, not yet but I'm thinking it may just be stress. You know stress can make you late with your period," I define making up empty excuses.

"Sooo, don't you think you need to be going to the doctor just to check if you are pregnant and seriously, do you think you should be drinking wine?" CeeCee then asks with a goody-two-shoes way of making me feel.

"Boo, who knows, I'm just so stressed right now I just need something to help me relax. Besides, I've read that wine won't hurt a baby anyway because it's made from grapes."

"What kind of foolishness is that? What are going to do? Is this the reason the married guy put you out? Some men just don't want to be responsible for their actions."

"Actually no, that's not quite it, you know I told you I had another guy up in the loft and he found out about it and that is why he put me out."

"Honey, you can't be doing that, especially if it is his place and you guys' have an agreement. Was he just a friend or somebody you're actually in a relationship with?"

"I don't even know what Lenox and I have going on, but since Troy is married I get lonely from time to time and I needed me a friend and bam...there was Lenox. Besides, we both know him and have a relationship with him so I don't understand why he's even tripping."

"Wait a minute did you say his name is Troy? What's his last name?"

"Troy Wilkins, why, do you know him? He is loaded! He owns a few black magazines."

"I know who you're talking about, but no, I don't *know* him. How long have you guys been messing around with one another?"

"Ummm, a little over two years. Pretty much since me and you broke up. Well, actually, he is the reason we broke up. I'm so sorry for it to come out like this, but I was really diggin' this dude. He really stepped in my life at a time that I was in a world of confusion and I fell for him quick. You and I always seemed to be at it, we were arguing all of the time, not spending any quality time with one another, and the sex was almost non-existent.

14

"I guess it is safe to say now that we had grown apart. So anyway, he had the looks, money, power and charm, just about everything you could possibly want from a man accept he was somebody else's husband. CeeCee, what in the world have I gotten myself into? I'm more lost and confused than ever."

"Well, whatever you decide to do you already know that you will definitely have my support. So when are you going to the doctors?" asks CeeCee still being a worrywart.

"I really can't answer that. You know I don't have insurance and my mind has been in a time warp all week, I just haven't had the energy to stress about that, too!"

"We need to get you to a doctor so you can begin the pre-natal appointments. I'll make an appointment and I will go with you and I will pay for everything. Don't worry we will get through this together. I will just have to see about trying to add you to my health insurance, even if we have to lie."

"Thank you, CeeCee Carter, you are the best friend a person could ever have and I'm so sorry that I ever hurt you."

"Don't even worry about that, instead we need to worry about what you're going to do about this baby and your future."

"What do you mean do about the baby?" I curiously ask.

"What are you going to do about keeping and caring for this baby? Have you even thought about adoption or an abortion? How about getting a real job with benefits and stability? Have you thought about what part the father is going to be in you and this child's life?"

"CeeCee, right now I don't even know what today is let alone thinking about all of that. Give me some time to process all of this to even start seeing things clearly so maybe then I can make some smarter decisions than I've already made. You've given me a lot to think about in such little time, just give me some time to process everything. Can you give me time to do that?"

"Okay, I'm sorry. I guess I did come at you with a lot. Together we will work something out," CeeCee agrees, stroking my hair, as I'm loving resting on a strong, comforting lap.

CHAPTER 3

The Beginning of Strangeness

YODRA WILKINS...

I was awakened early Saturday morning by the ringing of the telephone. Just coming out of a sound sleep, the voice on the other end immediately made me nervous and freeze up like a deer caught in some headlights.

"What's taking you so long, Baby?" questions the anxious voice on the other end of the phone.

I held the phone in silence just to see if the other end had been picked up, too! When I felt assured that it hadn't and after glancing around the beautifully decorated room, I checked the time, then I spoke.

17

"Hey, didn't I tell you that I would call you when I got up and out?" I interrogate sounding a bit aggravated. "And why are you calling on my home phone anyway?"

"I called your cell phone a few times but I was so frazzled to talk to you and I want to see you now, Baby, I miss you!"

"I miss you too, but let me see if Troy has left yet and I'll call you back after I get out," I instruct not knowing if Troy was still home or not. Just as I got up out of my comfortable king sized ivory post bed, I heard the charm from the door and saw the indicator light on the keypad show it was from the back door.

"Yodra, are you up yet?" yells Troy.

"Yes," I shout right back at annoyed as I went into our private Spanish tiled bathroom.

Shit! He must not be playing golf today, I wonder why? He usually takes every opportunity he can to play golf when he's not traveling or working or messing around with all of those different women over the years. But this week he has been lollygagging around the house. Something is just not right, I ponder.

"Good morning, Mama," bursts in Ivory-Jade through the bathroom door. "I know what I want for my birthday now!"

"Well good morning to you too, Sweet Pea, and what might that be?" I curiously ask.

"I want some new clothes and shoes, an Ice Princess Charm bracelet, an iPad and a pool slumber party with a few of my best friend-girls."

"Wow, okay, Big Girl. Have you discussed this with your Dad?" I request inquisitively?

"Yes, and he said to tell you to take care of everything. I think this will be real cool seeing as though it will be in the middle of my two vacations, Mama. Can I have a back to school party, too?"

"Well, it's not every day that my baby turns eight years old is it? Okay, I'll see what I can do to make sure all of your demands are honored while you're in California with your grandparents. As for a back to school party I will have to think about that, okay?"

"Okay…but why will you have to think about a back to school party?" she asks with a unmotivated tone.

"Because, I don't know what I may be doing is why. My life does not just stop because you want something done right now, Sweetheart. I will have the birthday party and that is for certain, but like I said, I am going to have to think about a back to school party.

"Did you forget about my art unveiling? It will be the same week that you will be home. You know, in between your vacations. It's already going to be a lot on me during that time and now I will still have to plan this illustrious party for you, too!" I respond while acting like I was going to faint.

"Yes, Ma'am, I'm sorry, I'm just excited and I really want everything to be just right, is all. What exactly is an art unveiling anyways?" she asks curiously.

"Well, I will gather what I think are my best photographs, have them framed and put on display for others to see. It's a very exciting time for me and I wanted you to be there to share this important moment with me. I purposely planned the unveiling the week that you will be home for your birthday."

"So people are just going to look at it and stuff?"

"Yes, and critics will critique them as well as I will have an opportunity to network socially and introduce myself as a professional photographer to the world."

"That sounds pretty boring if you ask me. Why would you care what other people say about your photos anyway? Didn't you tell me that if you did your best then you should take pride in your work and not worry about what other people say as long as you like it?"

"True, but when you're creating art and displaying it you want to hear what people have to say about it. The more people that like it the more opportunities I will have to showcase my art in galleries as a respected and professional artist. Now go get ready so I can drop you off at the airport. I packed all of your stuff last

19

night so all you'll need to do is get dressed and have your Dad put your things in the car."

"Well I'm proud of you and I like your photos even if nobody else does," she exclaims giving me a nice, tight hug. "You want daddy to put my bags in the Rover or the BMW?" she questions before leaving the bathroom.

"You know I don't like driving your dad's gas guzzling Rover, so you don't ever have to worry about asking me that again."

"Okee dokee," she answers as she skips out of the bathroom into my bedroom, bumping into her daddy.

"Good morning to my two favorite, beautiful ladies," Troy announces as he was enters our bedroom, grabbing Ivory-Jade up in his arms and giving her a big bear hug.

"Good morning, Daddy!" Ivory-Jade exclaims with an excited look on her face she always has when she looks into her daddy's eyes. "I told Mama what you said about my party and she's going to get right on it," she informs him hugging him again on the way back to her room to get ready.

"Oh yeah, mama asks can you please put my bags in *mom's* car?"

"I sure can, my little June Bug," he answers.

"Good morning, Troy, you're not going to the country club today?" I probe trying to figure out why he was still the hell at home.

"I've decided to start spending some weekends at home with my family and just play golf once and a while, leaving business days and hours for conducting business. I realize I have been ignoring my family and I have been missing being a part of my two favorite ladies lives," Troy states with a sorry attempt to apologize for the years of ignoring us.

I can remember just yesterday he didn't seem to give a damn about me and Ivory-Jade and what either one of us had going on in our lives. It's a shame that all of Ivory-Jade's friends' parents think that I am a single parent and if it were not for her grandparents allowing her to spend the summers with them I wouldn't get any sort of break.

"Well, Ivory-Jade and I have a very, busy schedule for today so you'll be here by yourself, I guess? You do remember that she is leaving today to go spend the first three weeks of this summer with your parents?" I ask as I continue putting on my clothes.

"Already, isn't she too young to be getting on an airplane by herself? What if she gets scared? Who's going to watch her? Don't you think you should be going with her?"

"Wait…Troy; we've already talked about this. For an extra fee the airline has an escort policy for children so she actually won't be traveling alone she'll have an escort with her the entire flight. Ivory-Jade will be just fine and your parents are going to meet her at the gate in Los Angeles. She will be coming back the same way in three weeks. And you know she'll be home for just a week for my unveiling and her birthday party then back off to spend the last three weeks with my parents."

"I just don't think she should travel half way across the country without an adult being with her."

"Well, if you feel that strongly about it then why don't you go with her? You're the one so adamant about her not traveling alone. Ivory-Jade spends every summer with our parents and you knew well enough in advance to make arrangements to fly with her if that's what you wanted to do," I state trying to control my attitude.

"I guess if they have a policy in place then she'll be fine," he replies trying to step out of that pile of shit he just created. "Well, do you want me to at least go with you to the airport to drop her off?" he asks.

"No, thank you. That may not be such a good idea since I have other things I need to do today anyway. You'll just be bored and rushing me to hurry up, you know how you do."

"Are you sure? I cleared my schedule to hang out with you guys today and, Baby, I'm really trying to put forth the effort to show you I love you. I want so badly for us to work out, Baby."

"That's sweet and all, Troy, but just because you decided to *finally* put your family first does not mean that our world is just going to stand still and wait for you to catch up. We have already been doing our routine. You see, you and my family have always come first in my life and I've done nothing but want to make our marriage work.

"I think I can get her off just fine. I have an idea, why don't you go ahead to the country club and get a few holes of golf in, relax and just hang out with the guys for today," I encourage.

****

Troy and I met during our second year of graduate school and we were the "college sweethearts" most people envied. We had the best loving relationship, our drive for success was strong, our style for fashion was impeccable, and our over-all spirit for life was amazing.

We both hold business degrees in management with a minor in marketing, as well as graduate degrees in finance. Before even marrying we decided we would be the "power couple" and start a black fashion and business financial magazine. I am the CEO of the fashion magazine called Onyx Trends and Troy is the CEO of the business financial magazine called Onyx Financial Enterprises and it only took us two years to do it

We married right away but children were not on our immediate timetable. We wanted to live our lives as one for a couple of years and establish ourselves in the business worldwide as serious entrepreneurs. We wanted to enjoy the fruits of are labor and pat our selves ourselves on the back for staying focused and determined in college and not let excuses deter us from our long term goals.

We also wanted to finally enjoy the hard earned money we had finally produced. At least that honeymoon period lasted almost three years when we were blessed with our beautiful little angel, Miss Ivory-Jade, named after the colors at our wedding.

A Taste Of Honey   Ravry Sloan

I was so in love with this sexy, smart, talented, ambitious man. He was the complexion of sweet, dark chocolate with eyes so deep, dark, and sexy that they could make your panties wet by looking directly into them. He has always worked out so his body is very sculptured and defined. We used to make love all day, every day, everywhere. We were like rabbits, spontaneous and so attracted and turned on by each other. All of our friends were envious of us and our love attraction, we were *that* couple.

In the beginning Troy was very excited about being a husband as well as a new daddy, but that all soon faded with the global success of our magazines.

By the time Ivory-Jade turned two years old Troy was spending a lot of time at the office, then he started going on business trips, then even longer, more frequent business trip, which led to him tapping into the real estate industry.

Troy was on top of his game and became a reputable, corporate businessman, as well as a successful magazine owner and CEO. I've contributed just as much money to our household accounts as he has, but money, power, and control is all Troy seems to be obsessed with.

Troy wants to seek, conquer, and destroy his prey. He will hunt to see who is the weakest. He will stalk to see when they're at their weakest. Then pounces when they least expect it. After that he simply walks away with absolutely no concerns or after thoughts about what he just did.

Although this is how this man is I love him, always have, and probably always will. The downfall is we are just so disconnected now that I think there may never ever be an opportunity for us to reconnect. Having a baby outside the marriage also didn't help with the bond, but I've accepted it and it is what it is.

None-the-less, in Troy's frequent absences I have picked up an exciting hobby, photography, and I am a buzz among some of the world's best photographers. Some of my art has even been displayed in some highly respected museums. I have met some amazing people who can really help me take this little hobby of

23

mine off the ground to the next level, including the famous photographer CeeCee Carter. Who just happened to agree to be my mentor and special friend, among other things.

As a matter of fact, I have my first sponsored art show later this summer to reveal my own collection. I'm so excited about this event. I will have spoken word, a live jazz band, an open bar, and light hors' devours. Now all I have to do is narrow down which pieces I will make known as well as have them framed.

Troy doesn't think I should have any outside interest as long as Ivory-Jade is still young. Sometimes I think he's right because I want to cherish these growing, impressionable years, but I'm no fool, I know what Troy is up to. He just wants to make sure I'm at home while he's in the streets being a man whore, but for now I'll let him think he's won this little game.

Actually getting caught up in his little discretion in the past I think made our marriage turn into that of convenience and stability only. We seem to not enjoy each other's company anymore and other than an event that the press is present. We don't even do anything together as husband and wife, or as family for that matter anymore.

I married for companionship, to feel needed and loved, to be appreciated, to be happy, and to be respected. I need to look into someone's eyes and feel the love that's in their heart. I need to laugh with someone, to dream with someone and Troy stopped doing the things I fell in love with him a long time ago.

I love my husband and want nothing but for us to be happy and live happily ever after, but I had to fill my loneliness...my emptiness...my longing to be loved.

CHAPTER 4
Havoc on the Greens

TROY...

The 45 minute drive to the country club gives me the incentive to contemplate the situations I keep putting myself in. Everything got out of hand but it's time that I try to make some major life changes for the sake of my marriage and my future.

I really have all I need at home. I have a beautiful, loving, loyal wife and the mother to my adorable daughter.

She always supports and encourages me in setting goals and reaching my dreams. And she has been forgiving when it comes to my indiscretions.

In other words, I need to get my shit together before I mess up my good thang and my good life! Starting right now Yodra and Ivory-Jade will be everything to me; they will be my life, my

25

reason for living. I should have made this commitment to not just myself, but to my family a long time ago.

As I pull up to the country club Bryce and Chance are standing outside where a lot of commotion was surrounding them.

"What's going on?" I ask as I give the keys to the Range to the valet.

"Troy, Man, we should be asking you that. Your little *piece* just came up here and causing major havoc, Man. What have you done to her? You need to handle your business, Bruh," explains Bryce.

"I don't know what you're talking about. What piece?" I deny the accusations without hearing more of the facts.

"That little hottie of yours, that stripper," clarifies Bryce in almost a whisper.

I turn around looking puzzled, almost in shock because I can't believe she lost her mind like that and actually come up here. "Wait until I get my hands on that little bitch!" I angrily speak through my teeth in a low tone that only Bryce and Chance can hear.

"Mr. Wilkins, Mr. Wilkins!" shouts Mr. Larks, the manager of the country club, running towards me.

"Yes, Mr. Larks," I politely respond turning towards his direction and making my face seem surreal.

"Mr. Wilkins, the management of The Buchanan Royals Golf and Greens Country Club would like to inform you that we are pressing charges against the young lady that was stalking you and was strategically capable of coming on the confides of the club to harass you.

"The young lady also destroyed thousands of dollars worth of equipment and property as you can see. You will be assured the strictest of confidentiality as well as adequate security from our company for any future undertakings at our club. We sincerely apologize in any way for not having the facility tightly secured and I personally guarantee your safety when you, or any of the guests, are on our premises."

"Thank you, Mr. Larks.   I greatly appreciate your cooperation and quick response to a very embarrassing situation. I had no idea what was going on here when I pulled up. I was just as shocked and surprised with all of the activity going on as anybody else.

"I would also like to apologize for something like this even making its way to your fine establishment.   Again, it's a very embarrassing situation and I appreciate your confidentiality in keeping this within the margins of our club," I state hinting for discretion.

"But of course, Mr. Wilkins. As far as our management is concerned this was an isolated incident and the situation has been resolved," he agrees with a firm handshake and wink solidifying the agreement of the unspoken words of secrecy.

As I try to not let anybody see the smirk on my face, especially Bryce and Chance, I thought, what just happened? How did Mr. Larks think this was a harassment or stalking situation? Well, if you look at it, it is, but where did that come from?

"Troy, you lucky dog, you," Bryce jokes while extending his hand for a handshake.

"I have no idea what you're talking about, B," I lie as I pull my hand back, smiling.

"Man, how in the hell did you get that bogus shit dismissed? How in the hell did you get them to apologize to you and by taking the blame for your craziness and your crazy ass bitch?" ask Chance.

I really didn't know what to say so I made it up as I went along.

"That's the luxury of being a platinum member of an all men's country club, Gentlemen", I indicate confidentially. "What goes on in the club stays in the club."

"Wow, I must admit that was so smooth. I have to give it to you, Bruh, you did that damn thang! And just think, Yodra will be none the wiser, how sweet is that?" Chance adds excitedly.

"Now that you've admired how the game should be played in action, let's go play a few holes and have a few drinks while I

27

whoop ya'll asses!" suggests Bryce as we were detoured to the other locker rooms because of all of the carnage that earlier transpired.

In the back of my mind I couldn't wait until I got my hands on that little bitch. Who in the hell does she think she is? The nerve of her coming to my country club and showing out with her ghetto ass.

Chance makes a very valid point, what if this did get back to Yodra? How would I explain to her why Honey acted such a damn fool at the club?

Then I start thinking, what if she really is pregnant and it is my baby? My marriage would be over for sure this time! There is no way possible that is my baby, not after what she did.

Yodra forgave me one time but to do it again will be like a cancer to my family. That hoe' has probably been f*cking so many dudes all up and through that nasty ass strip club anyways. I just happened to be the fool to get trapped.

Damn that Honey's ass! She better be glad her ass is in jail right now or I would be over there stomping a hole in her ass right now.

CHAPTER 5

Change of Plans

YODRA...

As Ivory-Jade and I pull up at the airport I can sense her nervousness, knowing she will be flying alone. And just the sheer excitement of going to see her grandparents is definitely adding to it.

I thought about the much necessary break and spending some much needed quality time with Corbyn.

"Mama, are you going to miss me?" asks Ivory-Jade with a pretend look of sadness on her face.

"I sure will, Sweet Pea! You mean the world to me and I just don't know what I am going to do without seeing your lovely face every day."

"Do you want me to stay with you? I don't have a problem staying with you, you know?"

"No, Ma'am, you are going to California and you should really enjoy your visit with your Grandma Lois and Grandpa Joe. They miss you so much and they are really looking forward to spending these next three weeks with you.

Besides, you don't want to make them sad do you?" I assure her with guilt.

"Okay, Mama, I'll go just as long as you promise to take care of Daddy and my birthday party."

"Okay, Sweet Pea. Please be a big girl and behave yourself as you know you are supposed to do. And when you come home from California we'll have this extravagant birthday party for you as promised. Then...right after that you'll be off to finish up your vacation with your Grandma Kimble and Grandpa Xavier in Florida?"

"And school starts right after that, huh?" she asks.

"Correct. You are going to have another very exciting summer, Ivory-Jade! Do you know how many kids wish they can say they can spend every summer with their grandparents doing exciting things and going to different places? So there is no need for you to worry your pretty little head about me or your daddy and your stinking little party, okay?" I respond with a tickle on her neck with my nose.

"Okay, don't forget to invite Emerson and Loli and Ashli and Davis and Landon and..." she begins excitedly calling out a list of her friends names when I cut her off.

"I know, Ivory-Jade, I know. I have the list you printed out for me with their e-mail addresses and cell phone numbers in its entirety remember?" I state, holding up the long list of names she already has in my purse.

"Okay, now I'm excited, Mama!" she exclaims.

"Now, let's get going just in case we run into any obstacles getting you checked in and finding your designated escort for the trip. And again, as we already talked about, don't give this flight attendant any problems. You have enough stuff to keep you occupied and snacks when you get hungry."

"Yes, Ma'am, I'll remember. But what if the escort is mean?" she asks trying to find something wrong.

"I'm sure she won't be mean, especially if you're behaving. Let's not create the bad, let's just deal with reality, okay?"

"Okay, okay, I'm ready I guess."

"Okay, I'm really going to miss you and I love you so much, Sweet Pea. I know I said it already but please, please, please be on your best behavior when you're with Grandma Lois and Grandpa Joe. Don't let them give me any bad reports about your attitude and don't forget to clean up after yourself. Be helpful to them and polite, okay? And you know I love you Ivory-Jade," I express feeling a little anxiousness about her flight now.

"Okay, okay. I love you back, Mama." she responds, giving me a great, big hug and kiss as we walk into the airport.

After getting Ivory-Jade all checked in and finally convincing security to allow me to walk with her to her gate and sit with her until her plane boarded, I'm finally off to spend some much needed time with Corbyn.

I look at the screen on my cell phone and see that it is Corbyn calling again. Right on time I was though.

"Hello, Sexy," I greet as I answer the cell.

"Hey, You! First of all please let me apologize for the way I sounded this morning. I've been thinking about you all day, missing and wanting to be with you. When will I get to spend time with you today?"

"I just dropped Ivory-Jade off at the airport and I have a few errands to run, but I'll be right over after that. How about I almost couldn't get away today, but I'll tell you about it when I get there.

"Well, I have something I need to talk to you about as well," Corbyn notifies.

"Uh oh, is it bad news or good news?" I ask.

"I don't think it's bad or good news, just news. We'll talk about it when you get here and I love you."

"Okaaay," I say hesitantly, "and I love you back."

I wonder what in the world could it possibly be, I thought after hanging up the phone.

As I look at the cell phone screen in the deep thought the vibration in my hand brought me to reality. It was Troy, what in the world does he want? I remember when I couldn't get enough of this man, now I've had just about enough of him

"Hello," I answer sounding aggravated.

"Hey, Love of my life, can I take you out on a date?" he requests trying to sound romantic.

"Hey, Troy, I'm sorry but like I told you this morning I have plans for today," I answer in a matter-of-fact tone.

"You have plans all day? You can't make time for your hubby?" he asks sounding disappointed.

I release a sigh because the thought of spending time with him now just makes my body squirm. The only time he spends time with me is if the cameras are around. Why all of a sudden now I had to ask myself?

"Sure, Troy. What about later this evening?"

"Great, Babe. Around 10:30, 11:00?"

"That's fine, Troy. What are you up to?" I ask sounding kind of puzzled.

"I just think it's time that I realize that you and Ivory-Jade are my priority and it's about time I start to take advantage of that. Is something wrong with me wanting to spend time with my beautiful, sexy wife?"

"No, I'm just in shock that you are so *adamant* about *wanting* to spend quality time with me today of all days. Either way, count me in and I guess I'll see you tonight then, okay?"

"Okay, Love...and, Yodra, I love you, Baby," expresses Troy being obviously sincere.

What in the world is going on? Troy rarely tells me he loves me.

I wonder if he knows about Corbyn. Now I'm not only worried but I'm nervous.

I wonder if what Corbyn has to talk to me about is about Troy. As many indiscretions Troy has had on me I know he should charge anything I do to the game. He owes me that much, plus you can't really say that I am cheating per se, unless emotionally attaching is cheating?

A Taste Of Honey   Ravry Sloan

CHAPTER 6
The Proposition

HONEY...

I can't believe I've been pushed this far. I think I am seriously having a nervous breakdown or something. What in the world is wrong with me?

I've been dumped by a man before but why is this one affecting me this way? I've been locked up before but this time it feels different. I'm more embarrassed this time and I feel like pure trash. I feel like payback is definitely in order and it's taking over my thoughts.

"What are you locked up for?" questions this gorgeous, masculine type lady with long, thick braids.

"For making a complete ass out of myself, that's why!" I explain with embarrassment.

35

"You made an ass out of yourself? Let me guess, for a man, huh?" she investigates.

"Yeah, a man I actually loved and thought loved me back," I explain trying to hold back tears.

"Well, Boo, they'll do it to you every time. You don't need a man. You're too pretty and fine to allow a man to whip up on you like that."

"I didn't say he whipped up on me." I petition as I got up to walk around because of my anger.

"You didn't have to, I can see his *love* all over your neck," she states coming up behind me and grazing the back of her hand on my neck.

"Well, it's not like I didn't deserved it to some degree. I really am the one who f'cked up a little bit, tho'! I pushed him to do this to me. I never should have had another dude up in his shit. But I still didn't expect him to re-act quite this way."

"Damn, Ms. Lady that was kinda' f'cked up. By the way my name is Nukita Fontaine but you can just call me Nuki.

"I got caught riding a little under the influence of alcohol, so *they* say. I know I was straight. I know how much alcohol I can drink. I'll just get my lawyer to take care of this bullshit. What's your name, Boo?"

"Honey Sinclair, or should I say, better known as the idiot that just messed up a good thing. I was the sweet piece of ass on the side for Mr. Troy Wilkins living a perfect life until a week ago. Can you believe that?" I blurt out his name accidently from all of my frustrations.

"Troy Wilkins the big time money man?" she asks.

"Yeah, you know him?" I examine now wanting to kick myself for saying his name out loud.

"Not really, but my brother does business with him from time to time. I heard he was like stupid rich."

"Yeah, he is. He owns tons of property and the Onyx Magazine lines."

"Oh, *he* owns Onyx Trends and Onyx Financial Enterprises magazines. I could have sworn a couple owned it," she states.

36

"I know you don't mean his soon-to-be ex-wife? That bitch don't own shit! Troy told me all she likes to do is live off of his hard earned money. She doesn't even want to satisfy him in bed like a real woman is supposed to."

"And you do?" she queries pissing me off by her tone.

"Yes I do and have been for about two years now if you must know! What we have is real!"

"And that makes you feel like a real woman? All you are to him is a sweet piece of ass; nothing more. But the little wifey has the respect, the title and the man. Now how exactly does that make you feel, again?"

"I don't owe you any explanations because my business is my business."

"True, true, but maybe you should do a little research on the man you're f*cking so you don't look and sound like a complete ass all of your life. She is in fact part owner of those magazines with him, as well as a couple of other successful businesses.

"Have you seen her? She is gorgeous! Now she's the kind of woman any man or *woman* would love to have on their arm. Google her name and you'll see how important she is to the business world and her community. That man will never leave all of that for you, and nobody else for that matter.

"Oh yeah, just in case you didn't know they have also been voted Atlanta's Couple of the Year. So again I say, he ain't going nowhere, Boo."

"You think you know so much? Troy is the bread winner in that family and he told me that she is just with him because of his money and fame. She's the wife so of course she's going to be mentioned but she is nothing more than just his wife. He's just trying to figure a way to get out of that nightmare and so she won't take half of his money," I shouted.

"And you think you're going to just get it because you're f*cking him? You think his wife is not going to get anything from their marriage?" she tests me again sounding just as cynical as before.

Out of pure frustration and loss of control, and before I knew it, I hauled off and spit in her face.

"Bitch f'ck you! You don't know me like that. And for your information Troy and I are in love!" I scream at her.

"Wow! You know most bitches would be so f'cked right now?" she indicates as she smoothly wipes my spit off of her face.

"I know you really don't know me, but I'm going to give you a pass on this just this one time. I won't even do you like that, this time. I like you too much. I like your fire. Why don't you let me put it out? Let me get a taste of that sweet honey," she aggressively states as she tries to grab at me around my waist.

"Bitch, I wouldn't waste my time with a broke 'hoe like you," I angrily say pushing off her advances.

"Oh don't get it twisted, Mz. Lady, best believe I ain't broke by no means. I bet I can treat you better than that nigga or any other nigga out here in these here streets.

"I'm a very successful owner of Charmed Escort Services, all legit and all mines. Don't let the smooth look fool you or the fact that I'm a little rough around the edges but I'm a very successful business woman. I have connections all around the world—from athletes to entertainers, from actors to top politicians, from business owners to doctors and lawyers--the list can go on.

"I'm recognized all over the city for my business mind and success. That's how I know about Troy and his wife's success.

"I bet you're intimidated of a woman like me, huh? You couldn't handle a woman like me and if you're scared just say so. I can respect that better than just being bitchy or childish," she propositions me in a condescending tone.

"I ain't scared of nothing and nobody for that matter. I'm just not interested," I protest.

"I can offer you more than any nigga will ever give you. When you get out come look for me. You can always find me at Splitz in Lithonia.

"You know, I let you get away with spitting on me which to some is considered the ultimate form of disrespect. You might want to get at me when you get out this thang just because I didn't whoop your ass.

"I know you're a struggling stripper, you don't even have to say it, I just know. You look like a stripper, you smell like a stripper, and I bet if you give me a chance you'll even taste like a stripper. I know what you like, I know what you need. When you get out why don't you come and get at me, Boo, I'm for real."

"Why would I want to do that?" I now ask with a little less resistance.

"Because, you know I got you, Boo. You know you're a good piece of ass and I can take real good care of you," she again propositions, walking up behind me, but this time gently kissing me on the back of my neck. She wraps her arms around my waste, pulling me closer into her.

"Hey, Big Nuki, back off of the inmate," shouts the guard doing her routine cell check.

"Honey Sinclair, come with me, it's time to get you processed," interrupts another guard.

"Bout damn time," I reply sounding annoyed.

"Hey, Honey Sinclair, get at me when you get out, Girl. I'll take good care of you," Nuki defines, blowing me a kiss as I walk out of the cell.

That damn Troy Wilkins has played me for a real damn fool for real this time! He was just making a fool out of me by using and controlling me with his manipulation and his charm.

I see now that he never really had any intentions on leaving his wife for me. It has absolutely nothing to do with money. It seems to me that she makes just as much as he does so he could have left her a long time ago. I've been sitting back waiting on him like a damn fool for two damn years and he's lied to me the whole damn time. I will be a fool no more.

CHAPTER 7
An Unhappy Ending

YODRA...

The rest of my day built up anticipation of spending quality time with Corbyn. It's been about a week but it seems like forever.

I'm glad that the special gift I ordered for Corbyn came in today! This is perfect timing for a morning that started off kind of strange.

I am feeling a little frisky so I stop by the store and grab a bottle of wine to get the mood started. I may as well get a tray of fruit and cheese in case we work up an appetite for a snack, I thought mannishly.

There is my baby's sexy, black bike pulled in the parking space at an angle. Maybe we can take a ride and get off some of this frustration later.

A Taste Of Honey   Ravry Sloan

Corbyn really thinks I'm *hott* when I wear dresses that show off my legs. I personally think it's for easy, easy access.

"Oh, my damn! You look so damn tasty," cries out Corbyn after opening the door.

"Thank you, Sexy, and look at you!" I state as we begin a slow, passionate kiss.

As usual, Corbyn's hand went immediately between my legs.

"Wait, wait, wait…let me put down this stuff first," I indicate almost dropping the bags to the floor.

"Then you better be putting them down then dammit and come back and give me some of that. I've been thinking about you all day. You've already made me wait long enough as it is, come here. Ump, ump, ump…this is exactly what I want," Corbyn indicates by cuffing my sweetness.

I barely turn around to place the grocery bags on the kitchen bar when Corbyn comes up behind me. And in a tight embrace, begins passionately kissing me on the back of my neck. Feeling the gentle pressure caressing my breast with one hand and the aggressive rubbing of my sweetness with the other hand, causes my body to melt and my sex to tingle.

I reach around and grab Corbyn by the back of the head, arching my back and thrusting this hotness with an invitation for some stimulation and a little tickling.

"Damn, Baby," is all I can say as two fingers ease quickly inside of me and immediately finds my g-spot.

I can no longer control the euphoria of bliss as my love juices ooze down around Corbyn's fingers. The fast repetition of internal throbs causes an extension of release. I spun around throwing my leg around Corbyn's waist, thrusting for some deeper penetration.

"It's about me making sure you're satisfied right now, you can take care of me later, how about that?" Corbyn whispers in my ear.

My body shutters from a quick, fast experience of delighted ecstasy.

"You must have been ready for me, Baby?" Corbyn says tasting me off of the two glistening fingers.

"Yes!" I answer feeling satisfied and a bit disappointed at the same time.

"Damn you taste so sweet."

"You know how you get me so hot and bothered I can't even help myself. Your touch is enough to send my insides on fire. Damn!" I explain trying to get myself back together.

"Damn, is right. Baby, you can't just be coming up in here teasing me like that. You know this is my favorite dress and you know that your scent turns me on."

"All I did was walk in the door, that is you who attacked me," I jokingly state acting like I am defending myself.

"Now, you already know I'm curious to know what you have to tell me, so do you want to sit on the rooftop or the balcony? Also, I have a surprise for you," I croon like I was singing a song.

"Let's go to the rooftop because I have a little surprise for you, too! I can't wait to see your face; you're going to love it. Oh yeah, before I forget let me go ahead and grab the iPod. I already know how you like your jazz," states Corbyn thoughtfully."

"I'm sure I will," I answer as I was led to the rooftop studio.

"I guess now you'll turn into the talented CeeCee Carter, the famous photographer and artist, huh? I still don't understand how you can become two different individuals by the mere mention of a name. To me Corbyn Carter and CeeCee Carter are one in the same, a sexy, talented photographer?"

"CeeCee Carter leaves some ambiguity as to the gender of the artist and of the craft. I want people to just love my work because it's beautiful. I am speaking through the windows of my soul, telling my message the way I'm feeling at that moment.

"Who cares if I'm a woman or a man, just enjoy the art. I want people to appreciate what I've done artistically and not judge it because of who I am."

43

"Well, personally I think that Corbyn could have been used as an ambiguous name just the same."

"But it sounds gendered to me, defeating my purpose. CeeCee is not a woman or a man it's just sounds like initials with no identity."

"Okay, if you like it, I love it. It's cute. It's like you have two personalities or something. If that's the inspiration to create such inspiring photographs and visual art then continue being CeeCee Carter.

"Honestly, that's the place where I'm trying to get to with my work. I want to get to the same level of beauty and imagination that you are on. I want my unveiling to be as memorable as your art."

"Trying to get to? You are already there, Baby! I've been trying to open you up to the beauty from your soul not the physical beauty from the surface. You have to clear your mind and thoughts and let your essence lead the way. If I can believe in you then you need to also believe in you."

I was in awe over the beautiful new pieces that were displayed all around Corbyn's studio. There were gorgeous black and white photographs of nature leaned up against the walls and set up on the easels.

"You are brilliant! I do love them, Corbyn."

"Thank you, Baby. You were heavy on my heart when I took these. You've also give me new outlooks on life, so with that being said, I am dedicating this entire collection to you and I'm calling it Raw Passion Collection."

"I love it! This is the best surprise ever! Thank you Corbyn, or should I be thanking CeeCee Carter?" I lightheartedly say while wrapping my arms around her neck and stealing some tender, juicy kisses.

"Uh oh, don't start something you can't finish," she expresses as she starts kissing me lightly in my ear.

"Okay, okay, okay I won't start because I'm too anxious to find out what you have to tell me. And I have to give you your surprise, too! We can have *playtime* later so let me run down stairs and bring up the stuff I brought."

"Do you need any help?" she caringly asks.

"Yes. That will keep me out from making two trips, plus I don't want you out of my sight, so come on, Darling," I state as I grab her hand and put it over my shoulder as we walk downstairs.

"You know I'm going to need your help for my unveiling. I will need the direction and expertise from the famous CeeCee in choosing the best photographs to tell a story. Will you help me?

"But of course, anything for you, Love. It shouldn't be that hard anyway because you already have an eye for visual expressions. Just let me know when you're ready and I'm on it. By the way, did I tell you how sexy you look today?"

"Ummm, I don't believe you did. So why don't you tell me again" I answer as we both laugh, unable to keep our hands to ourselves.

"You look very sexy my little Yodra Bear."

"Thank you, my little Corbyn Bear," I playfully echo after grabbing the gift and the mood essentials.

We then exit back to the rooftop. I set everything up on the beautiful stone table and light some romantic candles. I pour some Chardonnay and put on the jazz. We snuggle next to the outside fountain as I reveal my special gift.

"Oh, my, goodness!! This is so nice! Wow, is this silver?" she asks with the look of glee on her face.

"No, it's platinum and the case is made of genuine Coach Leather embossed with your name. I had my personal jeweler make this custom artist tool kit especially for you. Do you also see your name is engraved on the handles?"

"Yes, this is nice, Yodra, thank you so much! This must have cost you a fortune?"

"There is no price I wouldn't pay for the look of happiness that is on your face right now. I do have to warn you that the blades are as sharp as a surgeon's scalpel so you have to be very careful not to cut yourself or your canvas.

45

"My jeweler said he just could not understand why I wanted something so sharp just for paint, but who cares, that's what I wanted. Now that I've gotten that out of the way, I'm dying inside to hear the *news* that you've been so patiently waiting to tell me."

"No, wait a minute let's back it up a second. First things first, what is it you want to tell me about earlier today?" she ask.

"Oh yeah, let me tell you, why is Troy on this kick of wanting to spend time with me. Can you believe that? He actually wanted to go with me to drop Ivory-Jade off at the airport."

"You've got to be kidding me, for real?"

"Yes, and that is exactly what I said. Who knows, Baby? So, he's talking about he needs to spend more time with his family" I state with a serious tone and look on my face.

"Apparently something must have happened in his life to make him realize and want to pay attention to the queen he has had at home all of this time. I thank him for slacking these past couple of months and for giving me the opportunity to get to know you on a deeper, more connected level."

"Exactly! I sometimes wonder what took us so long to get together romantically anyway," I calmly state while slickly changing the subject

"Awe maaan, you know I was into you, but you wanted to play hard to get," she enlightens as she play like she was pushing me away.

"Don't do me like that, Baby," I playfully state while folding my arms like I was mad.

"But for real, Corbyn, I know what we're doing is wrong. All of these years I've accepted being ignored and cheated on, now it's my turn to find happiness. I know two wrongs don't make a right, but sweet revenge taste so much better than the bitter truth of our marriage."

"His loss is definitely my gain, thank you Mr. Troy Wilkins. But what I want to talk to you about is about my ex-girlfriend Honey. You remember me telling you about her right?"

"Yes," I answer hesitantly not exactly sure if I want to hear what was to come next.

"Well, she came by last night and she was really in desperate need of somewhere to stay.

"First, let me start of by letting you know that there is absolutely nothing going on between Honey and I, she just needs somewhere to stay. She is still my friend and as you know I don't turn my back on friends," explains Corbyn.

"I see. So, is she here now?" I want to know thinking how embarrassed I would have been if she saw us in an intimate situation.

"No, she left earlier and I haven't heard from her since. I just want you to know and be comfortable knowing that I've offered to let her stay here until she gets on her feet. I hope this won't be a problem?"

"I hope not either, but what can I say? She's your friend and I know what kind of person you are. And you are sure that's it though, right?"

"I'm positive, Baby. I'm so into you right now that I couldn't even think of breaking your heart. Honey and I have gone through our fair share of heartache and disappointments and I never want to relive those moments again. She was young when we were together and I was lonely. I was her first lesbian relationship so those can be tricky kind of relationship anyway."

"I want to be jealous but I won't, I have to take your word. Besides who am I to talk when I go home to Troy every night? That has to be a lot for you to have to handle on a daily basis as well."

"It is, but I love you so much that I will do anything to be with you. I guess you have that effect on me," she says as we both laugh and begin to kiss when her phone interrupts us.

"Yodra Bear, I need to go and take this call, I'll be right back."

I watch her as she leaves the room, thinking what in the hell am I doing with a woman? This goes against everything I believe in. This would embarrass my family, humiliate my

47

parents, and shame my daughter, but I just can't help it. I can't control who my heart loves and who loves my heart back. She makes me feel like nobody has ever made me feel, loved.

"Yodra, I have to leave I'm so sorry. Honey went and got herself locked up over some foolishness and she needs my help. I'll have to tell you about it later, when the time is right. I told her to leave that dude alone, but she's so hot tempered and hard-headed," she says under her breath, tossing her cell phone on the chair.

"So, is this how it's going to be from now on? Every time she gets into some sort of trouble you have to be her savior and protect her by bailing her out of jail?" I ask provoked about this whole situation already.

"No, that's not it at all, Yodra. She just needs my help. I'm going to help her get her life in order, as much as I can, so please don't worry about her. She will not interfere with us, I promise."

"She already has. You can't make that promise because you don't know that, especially if every time she falls you have to be there to pick her up."

"I promise you, please take my word on this. Yodra, it is you I love and I just love her as a friend. Trust me."

"Fine! I'm going home and get ready for my date with my husband then!" I say harshly.

"A date? So now you're going out to spend some time with *him*? When did you decide to do all of this? Huh?" she asks as I see the pain in her eyes.

"Today, my husband called and asked could we go out this evening and I said yes."

"So you choose on your way out of the door to tell me this? And you said it all nasty to hurt my feelings. I don't understand? Why are you going out with that loser when you say you can't even stand being in the same room with him?"

"Because he is my husband, has always been my husband before I ever met you, and as for now, will always be my husband!" I answer and put a little stank on it.

"Damn, Yodra, I never predicted you to be so evil and to act this way. I'm shocked!"

"And I'm pissed! As soon as your ex-girlfriend calls you stop, drop and run to bail her ass out of jail and give her place to stay! I really don't understand that? Pretty much you're taking care of your ex-girlfriend, right? If she hurt you the way you said she did why would you even care? Why even be bothered?"

"I wish things didn't have to be this way, but I've told you before I don't leave my friends stranded, including Honey.

"I need for you to trust in what I'm saying and know that I truly love you. I really, really do but with all of that being said, I need you to leave. I need to go and post bail for my friend and you need to get ready for your date with your *husband*," she sarcastically states.

She walks right past me and holds open the front door, as if to say get the hell out.

"Well, I guess that is that, huh? Bye!" I shout as she slams the door behind me.

CHAPTER 8
Uh Oh...

TROY...

Where could Yodra be? I'm actually very anxious and excited to spend some quality time with my wife. She always has a way of lifting my spirits and reminding me what's important and what I have.

This better be Yodra telling me she's on her way, I thought when my cell phone rings. Unknown caller is what popped up on the caller ID screen. Who in the hell could this be? Why do I have the strangest feeling that this is going to be Honey's ghetto ass on the other end of the phone?

"Hello?" I speak very slowly.

"Troy, we need to talk," Honey calmly requests on the other end of the phone.

"No, we don't need to talk. You made your bed now lay in it. It's over, Honey."

"Troy, I made a mistake, please forgive me," pleads Honey.

"You've made more than just a mistake. Why did you to the country club and show your ass? You embarrassed the hell out of me."

"I'm sorry, I wasn't thinking, Poppi. I just reacted, please forgive me?"

"You have lost your mind. What if my wife found out about your little breakdown?" I ask.

"I know, I know and I'm sorry. Please, Poppi, can we talk at least about the baby?"

"You want to talk about the baby? Now I know you've lost your mind. I told you before that is not my damn baby. You better check with that nigga you were f'cking up with in my shit, that's who you better talk to, not me. How dare you try to use that shit to get what you want from me!" I say screaming at this point.

"Troy, but this is your baby! I know how things might look and I admit I f'cked up, but this is your baby and you're going to help me take care of it," she then threatens as her tone changes.

"Oh, is that a threat?" I ask just to be clear with her intentions.

"Hell nawl, this ain't no threat, this is a muthaf'cking promise. You are not going to use me just to sleep with me and as soon as I make one little mistake throw me away like a piece of trash. I don't think so, Buddy.

"I just really don't understand what the big deal *really* is, Troy. You go home to a wife every night and what in the hell was I supposed to do up in that loft all alone?"

"If you're going to play the game learn to play by the rules, Little Girl. You really weren't ready for this major league shit and you messed up, now deal with it.

"Now, I'm done with you, Honey, and you can keep those damn baby stories to yourself. Now get off my phone, never call me again, and I don't want to ever see you again! And…and…one more thing, don't ever try pulling that bullshit trying to embarrass me again or else."

"Or else what, Mr. Troy Wilkins? Look muthaf'cka you're really not in a position to be the one cutting anybody off. You're the one who has more to lose than me so if I were you, you better watch yourself or else."

"Now, I've tried to be nice but, Bitch, please! Don't you ever threaten me or you'll wake up dead! Now trust and believe what I'm saying, Honey, you don't want to f'ck with me! I'm really not the one you ought to be trying to f'ck with! Just ask Juicy!" I was then shouting to the top of my lungs. I can hear the front door open so I hang up abruptly.

"Troy, are you okay?" yells Yodra from the foyer.

"Oh, I'm okay, Baby. I had to handle some business. You know how it is sometimes.

"I've been waiting on you, Baby," I express hoping to impress my baby, standing in the living room in a sea of roses.

I watched Yodra walk towards me seductively.

"What took you so long, Baby? I miss you," I say handing her a single pink rose and kissing her delicately on her lips.

"I had to run some errands, but I'm here now," she explains with some sort of resistance.

"Wow, you really look nice, where have you been?"

"Oh, me and the girls just spent the day together and went to an afternoon wine tasting."

"Damn, I can't wait to see how you're going to look for me tonight then if this is how you look with the girl," I say excitedly.

"Okay, give me about an hour to get ready," she informs while pushing me away.

"What's wrong, Yodra?"

"Nothing's wrong, Troy. I'm just tired and I have a lot of things on my mind. Where are we going anyway?"

"I was thinking about Café Chocolate. I heard they have some hot local talent."

"Oh, okay I've heard about that spot, too! So let me get freshened up," she articulates as she hurriedly runs upstairs.

A Taste Of Honey   Ravry Sloan

The house phone rings. I already have the feeling it was going to be Honey's ass. I yell to Yodra, "I'll get it, you just continue getting ready, Baby!"

"Okay, just take a message if it's for me."

"I will." I look at the caller ID and it was unknown number. I know she knows better than to call my home phone, I thought as I destructively answer the phone.

"Hello."

"So you thought you could just hang up on me and get away with it? Poppi, I ain't going nowhere until we can sit down and talk. I refuse to be just cut off like this."

I had to figure out something for this crazy bitch to not call the house phone back so I temporarily agreed to her demands.

"Look, Honey, okay we can talk. I'll call you later this week so we can meet," I forcefully agree to get her off my phone.

"I just got processed out of jail because that silly ass man from that country club that had me arrested. So, yes, I'm a little aggravated and bothered, but I promise I'm good. And we don't have to wait to meet. I want to see you tonight?" she asks.

"Either we meet when I'm ready to meet or we won't meet at all."

"Why? You must be going out of town or something. Your sweet Honey is missing you and just wants to see you, Poppi, that's all," she pathetically begs.

"Look, we are meeting to talk and that is all. I'm done with you and that is that. You know there are some people have died for less, remember that. Now, I said I'll call you later on this week and we'll meet then.

"I'm hanging up and I don't want you to ever call my home phone again. Do you hear me? I want, no I need you to hear me when I say this for the last time, so hear me and hear me good. Let this be the last time you ever call my home phone and I mean it from the bottom of my heart Honey!"

"I love you, Poppi," she quickly expresses as we hang up the phone.

The nerve of that damn girl, she knows she can really annoy the hell out of me sometimes. Now how am I going to handle this situation? The one thing I cannot have is for her to keep calling my house jeopardizing my marriage, I see know this is going to be a real challenge. This thing is bigger than I could have ever imagined.

"Oooh, Trooooy," Yodra came downstairs a few minutes later singing my name like she was a different person than she was when she went upstairs.

"I'm here at the bar, Baby." I answer as the sound of her voice immediately made my sex swell.

"Well…?" she solicits a response about her appearance as if she were posing for a photographer.

"My, my, my…you look so damn sexy, Baby," I reply putting my glass of wine down.

I walk over to my wife and gently kiss her on the curve of her neck, knowing that turns her on. I reach to feel her moistness and to my surprise she wasn't wearing any panties, causing my sex to now throb uncontrollably.

I look deeply within her in eyes with desire and delight. After letting my hands wander down the curves of her body, all I could say was, "Ooh-la-la!"

"I'm the luckiest man in the world knowing that all of this is all mine," I declare while accidently on purpose allowing my fingers to slip inside of her wetness. In the back of my mind I was wondering what has gotten into her, but for now I am not going to complain. I am definitely going to enjoy this moment.

"Thank you, Baby, and yes, this is all yours. I hope you're ready for me. You haven't made me feel like this in a long time, Daddy," she said in a feisty, freaky manner.

She grabs me by the back of my neck to assist in raising her sweet peach to be on my manhood. She kisses me from my lips to my neck, seductively grinding on my hardness. My sex grew extra stiff just remembering and knowing how good her lovin' is.

Yodra is usually so reserved, where is this freaky side coming from?

A Taste Of Honey   Ravry Sloan

"I've been waiting on you all day, you just don't know. I've been imagining touching your soft, hot body and kissing you on your neck, but thank you for *giving* it to me, Baby," I say barely able to speak.

She suggestively pushes me back on the sofa and unbuttons my shirt. She softly kisses me on my chest, tickling my nipples with her tongue. I was ready to get a taste of her peachy sweetness and ready to enter in her personal space.

"Do you want me, Baby?" I ask.

"Yes, Daddy, yes!" she says in her baby voice that turns me on even more.

"Can I have you now?"

"How do you want me, Daddy?" she asks which seem to always runs chills up and down my spine, causing me to throb even more.

She knows how I like this little submissive game we use to play. It's been a long time since we've played it. I've missed it and I've missed her.

"You know how I want it, Yodra. Take care of your Big Daddy the only way a wife knows how to do," I order as she straddles across my legs.

She begins by kissing slowly down my stomach licking my ripples, while stroking my hardness with her soft hands. I just put my hands behind my head and looked up towards the sky because I knew she was about to take me to heaven.

I imagine my beautiful, sexy wife freaking me like this every day and there wouldn't be a need for "playtime" with Honey or any other woman for that matter.

"You're going to experience part one of this journey now and part two after dinner, just like the good old days," she states as she gently kisses the tip, stroking me up and down with confidence and teasing my hardness with her tongue.

"You like that, Big Daddy?" she asks, looking over my stomach and chest to look directly in my eyes.

She escalates my excitement by continuing to kiss and lick the tip.

"Are you ready for it?" she asks.

"Yes," is all I could say as she then permits all of me to slide in her spicy mouth.

I enjoy feeling the gentle pressure of her tongue slipping up and down my firmness. Her mouth squeezes tighter and tighter as she tastes me with great appreciation. Her hand strokes enhance the sensation of her mouth pleasing me. She only stops, momentarily, to slurp the wetness off the sides of me. Oh how I love that sound!

My heart pounds fiercely, my toes curl, my will to hang was on was no more. I try to push her back to gain some type of control of the eruption but her thirst for my firmness was powerful. She enters me deeper and deeper while she jacks my hardness wilder and wilder

All I can do is growl and prepare my body for a violent escape from the years' worth of build-up I held on to. I could feel the beast within rear its ugly as I lost the fight to stay in control.

Time stood still as I black out from the pure satisfaction of real love. I could feel the warm explosion ooze from her mouth as I try to gather the strength to come back to reality.

"Whew!" I scream feeling like I just conquered the world. "Thank you, Baby, I needed that! I've really been missing you and I apologize for neglecting you, but I've felt neglected as well," I express.

"We've both are very much guilty and I apologize for that, too! What happened to us anyway? Where did things go so wrong?" she asks with real compassion in her eyes.

"Baby, I wish I knew. Our lives have been so disconnected for some time now and we've both accepted it and allowed it to go on for so long. We've being glorified roommates and parents to Ivory-Jade only. But now that we've addressed it, what are we going to do about it?" I ask truly missing the closeness my wife and I once shared.

"We definitely need to communicate better and spend quality time with one another. And I don't just mean for business and social appearances, either. I've really missed you but your many indiscretions did not help us and that made trusting you that much harder," she states bringing up old stuff.

"Let's not talk about the past, let's move forward. First, allow me to apologize for not being trustworthy to you and for neglecting your needs. I've ignored my responsibilities to our daughter and to our marriage and I'm willing to re-build what we had," I sincerely express really ready to move past this subject.

"Troy, I use to think that what we had was just not worth the fight, but because you're willing to put some energy back into us then I'm willing to fight for us, too! This is a start and I want my husband back! I want my marriage to work!" she shouts with tears flowing down her crooked smile.

As much as I love Yodra how can I truly be loyal to her if I'm not consistently, satisfied sexually?. How can I get her to fulfill my sexual appetite and keep my hunger for sex at home? This is going to be hard and very, very tricky.

CHAPTER 9

You Better Be Walking, Girl!

HONEY...

I really don't know what to do about this Troy situation, I thought looking in the mirror in CeeCee's guest room. I just know he can't get away with this. How dare he give me the world then snatch it all away. I'll make his world crumble under his feet if he keeps ignoring me and putting this little meeting off. I'll show him.

"Honey, who are you talking to?" asks CeeCee coming into my room.

"I'm talking to myself since I can't seem to get this fool to talk to me. I'm just not going to accept him taking everything away and walking away from me like this, CeeCee. I didn't make this baby on my own and I'll be damned if I won't get the help that I am supposed to get."

"Come on, Honey, you don't even know if you're even pregnant yet. But if you are, what exactly do you want from him? What are your expectations?"

"I want what every other pregnant woman wants, *him dammit*! I can just feel it, CeeCee. I just know I'm pregnant. I am one of those women who you can set your clock by every month. I'm never late so that's how I know something just ain't right!" I scream with humiliation and disappointment.

"I don't know why I'm trying to convince myself that I may not be pregnant."

"I would like for you to honestly explain to me your reasoning behind your thought process. Tell me why you think this is how it's supposed to be when the situation was what it was? I need to know where your expectations are coming from," CeeCee inquires as she lay down next to me on the bed, putting her arm around me.

"It's really not as bad as you may think. This is how the whole thing got started.

"Like I told you before it was right around the time that you and I were really catching hell with one another. That was right around the time when I started dancing at Pink Pussycats.

"One of the other dancers, Juicy, was kicking it with this dude who turned out to be a regular customer. This dude was of course Troy. And from what I saw he really took care of her but all she knew how to do was complain. And I mean all of the time.

"I didn't see him that way at all. I saw him as being a very handsome man, tall, chocolate and intelligent. He had money and appeared to me like he knew how to treat a lady.

"Over time he started shifting his eyes towards me and I already knew I had eyes for him so I didn't make it very hard. It started out subtle at first-- buying me drinks, requesting me for private dances and leaving me extremely *big* tips.

"But then we started hanging out after hours. He took me to dinners and on shopping sprees and trips. He soon started

60

wanting me all to himself so that's when he got me that loft and Escalade.

"Oh, CeeCee, he just made me feel so good, like I always thought a real lady is supposed to feel. He took me places I only dreamed about. Can you believe I have a passport and it's used?

"I've really gotten used to this lifestyle with no limits or limitations. He really made my life worth living. And this whole thing is really just a big misunderstanding. That's why I am having a hard time understand his behavior, nor will I accept it."

"A misunderstanding…really? How in the world do you see this as a misunderstanding, Honey?"

It's so much more to it than you know. But without knowing that, think about he has so much more to lose than I do. He's the one who is married. He's the one who is jeopardizing his family. He's the CEO and respected member in the community.

"But…he is also the cheater, a woman abuser, consumer of illegal substances and now he is getting ready to be a daddy to his lover's baby.

"But what's most embarrassing is that Troy has some real freaky fetishes and the biggest one is being swinger. We've traveled the world swinging with all sorts of people and we have a hometown couple. The guy was from that couple and that is what makes this whole thing a big misunderstanding.

"He won't even let me explain who the guy was up in the loft, or what was going on. That damn nosey ass doorman messed everything up.

"Troy has cheated on me and his pretty little wifey so many times and each time I've forgiven him. And check this out, he's also cheated with some of those tricks from the same damn club I was work in.

"And, let me just say this…he's gotten started with the guy before me and the wife could join them

"Now with all of this, tell me I don't hold the cards to play this game and win? I am the new dealer for this game and he better be ready to play or lose big time."

"I do not understand at all. This is really crazy how you have this all played out in your head," she expresses in a preachy kind of tone.

"It's not for you to understand, CeeCee; it's for us to understand. There are only two things that I know Troy values more than anything in this world and one is his image and the other is his family. Any distortion of this perfect image he has created will be a devastating blow for him and his ego and the threat of losing his family will destroy him as a man.

"I have the upper hand right now and he knows it. I'm sure I can get him to do whatever it takes to keep me from ruining his reputation and this from getting to his pretty little wifey.

"Besides, I'm not walking away with nothing that's for damn sure," I respond.

I then recall one night at the club Juicy telling us she had some proof that could really destroy Troy. She told us that he really wasn't the man he appeared to be. I haven't talked to Juicy in about six or seven months but I need to have a conversation with her, soon. Troy said to ask Juicy, I wonder what that means?

"Honey, are you still with me? Your mind seems to be wandering a little," CeeCee asks, snapping her fingers, as well as snapping me out of my temporary trance.

"No, I was just thinking about something, or should I say someone." I respond.

I really do think I need to talk to that girl Juicy, I'm sure she can provide some dirt on Troy and I have got to find out what that dirt is.

"I was going to say to you is you seem to keep referencing you, Troy and his wife as a mutual love triangle, have you ever met his wife?" inquires CeeCee.

"No, I never met her but I bet she's not even his type because I'm his type, short, sassy, hot, and freaky."

"Honey, you are a mess," she giggles as we both laugh.

"Yeah, but if wifey knew how freaky he really was she might want to get him checked out. She may even want him to start wearing a rubber. This guy really lives a wild life outside of their perfect little home.

"That's that image I'm talking about I want to destroy. The fantasy is that he's living--a perfect life, a perfect wife, a perfect daughter, a perfect business--but that's only the surface."

"Damn, that is very dangerous. Somebody could die because of his careless actions," she states worriedly.

"Now that I've revealed my crazy situation now you have to tell me about this mysterious woman who has stolen my woman's heart. Who is she? When am I going to meet her? What does she do?"

"Oh, Honey, now is not the time. Things are still very much complicated and I would rather just wait to explain it all to you when the time is right."

"I don't think anybody's life is as complicated as mine. Is it a man or something?" I ask curiously wanting to know what the big secret was about.

"Are you serious? I wouldn't waste my time dealing with a man and you know that. Excuse for judging but just look at this bullshit you're going through," she points out as we both laugh.

"Besides, I'm in love! And nothing can change that, even when we don't agree," she confidently states.

"Awwwe, that's great CeeCee, I should have stayed thinking that way then I wouldn't be in all of the confusing bullshit. You always treated me good and now look at me, just look at me, I'm a real mess. CeeCee, I'm about to have a baby! What in the hell am I going to do with a baby?"

"Honey, if by chance you are pregnant you do know you don't have to go through with the pregnancy. You do know that don't you? You can have an abortion."

"I know but I've never really had anybody to love me and I know a baby will, unconditionally. I need a golden ticket that I will always be taken care of by Troy and that he will always be a part of my life.

"I'm not like you, CeeCee; I can't make it out here on my own. I don't know how. I have to have somebody to build me up or I'm nothing. This baby will be that bond that I need and the leverage to get what I want without working hard for it at all.

"I'm tired of shaking my ass and dancing for tips. The sucking and f'cking on the side for a little extra cash is still not going to take care of me the way I want to be taken care of anymore. Like I said, I've gotten used to this life style and I refuse to go back to where I came from."

"Whatever it is you decide to do you do know you will have my support, one hundred percent. As I've told you before, I will express my concern for your future and the future of your baby, but I know the choices will be yours.

"I know that this may not be a real concern for you but I think you need to think about the quality of life and the future you can provide for this baby alone. This man is not going to break up his family for you. Every side piece has heard this before," she mockingly states.

"CeeCee, I'm kinda shocked to hear you be so concerned for a dude and his situation. What's gotten into you?"

"Nothing, Honey, I'm just saying. Did you really think this guy was going to leave his family for you just because you're pregnant?"

"Wow, so you think I'm a nothing too don't you? You think I get paid to f'ck and I'm not supposed to catch feeling or have dreams? You think I make childish decisions and I don't know right from wrong, don't you?" I annoyingly asks, running to the bathroom to cry out my frustrations.

"No, Honey, I don't think that, but you need to give this decision more thought than you've given anything else in your life. This is more life altering than any of the other decisions or mess up's you've made. This can't just be swept under the rug. This is serious and you need to be careful with how you think you can control other people and other people's lives and emotions.

"Come on back out here. I'm sorry to hurt your feeling but you needed to hear it and I needed to say it or I wouldn't be a true friend. Now, let's move past that moment and plan forward," her words comforting me to come back out of the bathroom and into her loving arms.

"CeeCee, I am scared and I really don't know what to do," I say sobbing hysterically in her arms. "But I don't want to look like a fool and feel as used as I do right now."

"I understand, but sometimes you have to get back up after falling down, dust yourself off, and pull up your big girl panties with confidence and you better be walking, Girl!" she awkwardly tries to demonstrate Beyonce's model walk, as she fumbles with the Bose radio next to the bed.

"You are so silly," is all I can say in between laughs and sobs.

"Come on, Honey, I said walk!" she shouts as she turns the music up and we strut around the bedroom.

We imitated models as if we were on a big runway at fashion week or something. And as always, CeeCee makes me feel as if everything is okay. My spirits lift up with every little step. I begin feeling like each step was a step in rebuilding me right back up to the person I am supposed to be.

A Taste Of Honey

Ravry Sloan

CHAPTER 10

What is a Girl to Do?

YODRA...

More than enough days have come and gone without me or Corbyn communicating with one another. I picked up the phone a few times to call her but my pride won't let me be the first one to call.

I'm also a little ashamed because I have let my guard down by allowing Troy to reconnect with me. This makes me so confused.

Troy and I have not had this type of loving union in years. Now all of a sudden he wants to act like we're all in love again. And I seem to be falling for it. We've always accepted a silent agreement as to how things are between us. Now he wants to change up the game and I am expected to roll with it.

A Taste Of Honey   Ravry Sloan

I am battling with this internal struggle of what I really want to do about me and Troy? What is best for me? What really makes me happy? I really do need to talk to Corbyn, badly! Better yet, I need to see Corbyn. I really do miss her so I guess I'll have to bend first after all.

"Hello," Corbyn answers as I can hear her fumbling with the phone.

"Hey, I need to see you and I need to see you now! I'm headed to Sips Coffee Café around the corner from you; can you meet me in a few minutes? I'm almost there."

"Sure, I need to take Scooter for a walk anyway so we'll be there in a minute or two."

"Good deal, see you in a few," I respond knowing I was already in the parking lot waiting.

"Are we going in or sitting in your car?" asks Corbyn startling me as she and Scooter walk up to the car a few minutes later.

"Let's just sit out on the patio since you have Scooter with you. Don't I even get a hug or a kiss or something? You're acting like you haven't even missed me," I state just wanting to feel her touch.

"I was waiting for you to get out of the car, Baby. Can we at least start this off friendly? We are friends right?" she asks looking unsympathetically in my eyes.

"Yes," I reply as I step out of the car, wrapping my arms tightly around her neck.

"I miss you, Baby," she sensually says in my ear as we hold each other.

I can actually feel her pain through her hug.

"I miss you too," I reply as emotions spill from my eyes down my face. "What's going on with us?"

"You're afraid of real love so you purposely allow a distraction to jeopardize your happiness. You jumped to conclusions about Honey so fast that I had to ask myself why? Maybe you have you fallen back in love with your husband and maybe you were just too afraid to tell me?" she expresses trying to fight back the tears of her own.

"All I've ever done is love you and want what's best for you. I will never hurt you or be unfaithful to you but you didn't believe me. I was completely honest with you about Honey but you jumped to conclusions and deliberately lashed hatefulness towards me. Now that I just don't and will never understand. Why knowingly attack someone? Why be so nasty?" she asks wanting answers.

"There is no good excuse for that and for that, Corbyn, I do apologize. But Corbyn, you're only seeing this through your vision, look at it from my point now.

"Your ex-lover comes back to you from out of the blue needing somewhere to stay because of *her* choices. She immediately gets into some type of legal trouble which you were expected to stop, drop, and go bail her ass out.

"Then you're taking care of her until she gets on her feet. I don't care what you say but she is coming before me and I am supposed to just be okay with all of that? You just want me to be accepting of the changes in our relationship and not question anything?" I detail.

"Yodra, you just jumped to assumptions and ran with it. You really didn't want to hear anything I was trying to say. Have I ever one time lied to you since we've known one another?"

"No you haven't, but..."

"No buts, have I ever lied to you or hurt you? Just truthfully answer that," she asks.

"No, but you know I've never had a relationship with a woman and I don't know how this is supposed to work. I don't know the rules. You once told me how in love you two were and how devastated you were when you broke up so I just assumed that when she came back those old feelings would come rushing back."

"Okay, I got that you may feel that way but why be so mean to me about it? Love is gender blind. Love is love, hurt is hurt, pain is pain, there are no different set of rules for us than for you and Troy. Why throw up in my face that you and Troy were

69

going out the way you did, why?" she questions obviously trying to fight back the pain she was feeling.

I sat there and couldn't do anything but cry. I hate I was causing her so much pain. This situation has forced me to confront that we are actually in love and this feeling is an overwhelming feeling. My marriage is complicated enough, but to be in love with a woman is an over-powering emotion that is controlling my heart.

"I didn't expect to fall in love," is the only thing I can think of to say.

"What? You didn't expect to fall in love? So what did you expect? You thought because I am a woman that I don't have feelings, that I don't get hurt, that what we had was not real?" she expresses walking away to get a handle of her emotions.

I sat there looking Scooter in the eyes, thinking what a funny looking dog he is with that under bite and poked out tooth. "Scooter, what am I doing? Just tell me the answers, Scooter," I playfully ask while stroking his head. He just laid there on my feet sniffing around for any crumbs that may drop.

"Yodra, I don't know what to say. I want to be done with you but I also want to be the one to make you happy. I know you haven't experienced real love yet because you married a jerk and you married so young. I don't know what to do about you sometimes, Yodra.

"Are you afraid of love? Are you afraid to love me because I am a woman? You know I won't hurt you don't you? Help me out or something, Yodra, because I'm hurting here."

"Corbyn, I don't know," I whine with frustration. "You're coming at me with all of this. I'm so sorry that this is hurting you because hurting you is the last thing I ever want to do," I barely utter trying finish my words.

"But..."

"But, Corbyn, I didn't know what to expect. You came in my life at a lonely, vulnerable time and you stole my heart. We connected on an intimate level though photography. You made it about me and yes, I did fall in love with you. But I have to be honest and say that is not what I was expecting. And this has

70

absolutely nothing to do with you being a woman either. I would feel this way if you were a man.

"Honestly, I was just looking to have my empty, lonely time occupied and I thought I may as well have some fun while I'm at it. I never expected you to be like this.

"I've always admired you from a distance. I think you are one of the most beautiful, talented women I know but what you bring to the table has really blown my mind and heart away. I'm caught up, Baby, I don't know what's next? I just don't know what to do," I tearfully confess as Corbyn knelt down in front of me to look into my eyes.

"Baby, love is not supposed to make you feel like this. It shouldn't be this hard to accept love. You shouldn't have to doubt the person who loves you and it should be easy to love them back. You should not feel stressed, confused, or even complication when in love.

"I feel as if I'm causing you more harm than good so I'm going to have to take a step back and just fade-away. As much as this hurts you it hurts me all the same, but I'm hurting you whether I'm here or not. I love you too much to cause you this type of stress and I love you enough to let you go."

I was in shock! I was speechless! I didn't have a plan for a future with us but I also didn't see it coming to an end, now or later. I am devastated! What am I going to do without Corbyn making me feel good about myself? How will I ever experience this kind of love again?

"So you're saying we can't be friends?" I ask not realizing my greediness.

"You are something else, Yodra. I thought friends' is what we already were until you decided to jump to conclusions about Honey and beat up my emotions with your words. I have to try and get a handle of what I'm feeling so just give me some time. I'm having a hard time grasping you wanting to make things work out with a man that treats you like a piece of shit, I just don't get it."

"Okay, Corbyn, I won't pressure you. Just know that you will be hard person to forget but I do respect you for giving me my space."

"I may give you some space to organize your heart but I'm not going anywhere. I'll always love you and don't be surprised if you see me show back up in your life. It's not going to be that easy to get rid of me for good," she states not blinking an eye like she was trying to scare me.

"You are so silly. I just don't want to lose a good friend that has seen the best in me and for that I am grateful!"

CHAPTER 11
The Sit Down

TROY...

I really don't want to see this damn girl right now. I swear, she is so full of drama. I already know she is going to act up and try to embarrass me. I was regrettably thinking as I pulled up at Café Intermezzo. I had to take a long, hard, deep sigh and get myself together to deal with this psycho and all of her drama.

"You're gonna stay in the truck the whole damn time?" Honey shouts as she pounds on my window after I parked the truck.

She seems to have just appeared because I didn't even see where she came from.

"Come on, Honey, I'm not with all of this bullshit today. Now we agreed to come here to talk and that is exactly what we are going to do. Do you mind letting me at least get out of the truck?

"Now maybe you can act a little civilized so we can go inside and sit down like two mature adults and talk like you wanted to do?" I calmly state walking right past her as if she didn't even exist.

"Poppi, you act like you don't even miss me. I thought you loved me?" she asks grabbing my hand attempting to put my fingers in her mouth and suck on them.

I snatch my hand back and kind of aggressively got up in her face ordering the rules of this lunch.

"Look, Honey, we are going to sit down in the restaurant and discuss whatever it is you want to talk about because I really don't have anything more to say to you. You will not loud talk me, you will not get violent, you will not embarrass me, and when I'm ready to leave I'm leaving. Now do you understand?"

"Yes," she replies with an uncomfortable look on her face.

I open the door and escort her inside while we wait for our table. "Where are you staying?" I ask.

"I'm staying with an old friend. You know, this has been extremely rough knowing we aren't together anymore. You don't miss me at all, Poppi?" she emotionally ask again.

"That's not the point and you know that. You broke the rules and these are the consequences you have to deal with."

"But, Troy, you won't even let me explain. See..." she began explaining when the server motioned for us to follow her to our table.

"You see that guy who came by the loft a few times was only Lenox. He and Loris had been having some problems and he didn't have anywhere else to go so I told him he could come there. I really didn't think you would mind. I was going to talk to you about it but before I could things really got out of control with the neighbors," she poorly tries explaining her stupid ass decision.

"How in the hell are you going to let another nigga come stay up in my shit regardless of what bullshit he has going on in his life? That nigga ain't my damn problem and he damn sho' ain't

74

your problem. But more importantly, what does any of that have to you do with you f'cking him in my shit? Those are the answers I'm waiting for and the only things I want to hear from you."

"Troy, are you for real right now? As many times as we've gotten together with Lenox and Loris and now you consider what me and Lenox did as cheating? P-lease!!! You've enjoyed both Lenox and Loris just as I have and you know exactly what I'm talking about."

"You just shut the f'ck up right now! What goes on behind closed doors is to remain behind closed doors and not to be discussed. Learn the f'cking rules to this game! That's what your problem is you don't know when to speak and when to shut the f'ck up!"

"Hold up, you can't be mad at me because the shit you enjoy you are ashamed of. Don't blame me for your down low fantasies becoming a reality. If my memory serves me correctly you and Lenox used to get started before me and Loris even came home. And not just one time but a couple of times, so don't tell me about no damn closed door shit!"

"Now you've crossed the line you little girl! I knew it was a mistake to come and try and talk intelligently with a dumbass. You sound as dumb as you are and I wish like hell I would give your dumb ass shit. You better figure out how you're going to raise this baby by your damn self and how to handle your own sorry ass pathetic life."

"Look muthaf'cka, I've been trying to be nice to your ass because I love you but I refuse to walk away from this shit with absolutely nothing. And for you to keep handling me like I'm a f'cking piece of trash is unacceptable.

"I'm tired of shaking my ass for a living and I will make your life miserable if you don't play this damn game by my new f'cking set of rules.

"I've been looking for Juicy and rumor is that you came and picked her up from Pink Pussycats a while back. And guess what? She hasn't been seen or heard from since. You better hope I find her because your ass will be going down if I don't.

"Now, get ready for the new rules. You will continue making sure that me and this baby are taken care of and that this baby will have the best medical care and life imaginable, just like your own damn daughter," she demands like I was going to agree.

"Honey, that's bullshit! First of all, the only time I ever saw Juicy was at the club so you better get those detective thoughts out of your damn head. Second of all, you just confirmed that you have officially lost your damn mind because I'm not doing shit because you say so or you threaten me. I'll rather go to battle with my wife than to bow down to your threats and demands.

"Now I'm going to politely pay the bill for our food then I am leaving. I kept up my end of the agreement, we met to talk and I don't ever want to hear from you again. Do you understand me?" I firmly confirm between my teeth trying not to draw any more attention to us than it already is.

"Troy, don't leave. Why do you want to leave? I'm sorry, please don't leave," she begs as she grabs my arm trying to force me to stay seated.

"Bitch, you've played with the wrong muthaf'cka this time. I'm not like those other broke ass niggas you f'ck around with in the streets and at that f'cking strip club. I'm a real goddamn man and you and no other bitch is going to make me do a damn thing! Get your damn hands off of me and let me go, now!" I shout.

"Okay, Troy, okay leave then, Muthaf'cka, leave! I don't need your ass but I promise you that your life has now entered the hell zone of Honey and I'm going to be on your ass. You better watch yourself now you hear? You just never know when I might show up in your dreams and cause yo' ass to live a f'cking nightmare."

"If you know like I know you better pack your shit and take your raggedy ass back home where somebody gave a f'ck about you. You don't want to keep f'cking with me, Honey, trust me you don't want to f'ck with me," I determinedly say panting for breath as I stood up to walk away.

"Wait, wait, wait, Troy, please don't leave me. Please, don't leave. I'm ready to talk for real now. I didn't mean any of

76

that shit I was saying please hear me out, please?" she again pleads.

I respectfully took my money out of my pocket and threw about a thousand dollars in hundreds at her ass and say before walking out.

"Take this and go start a new life so you can now get the f*ck out of mine. Honey, it's over! I don't give a f*ck about you and I could care less about that damn baby, so keep those childish games that you are playing to yourself, Little Girl, or go find a little boy to play them with you because I'm not that guy."

"Oh, so you're going to just disrespect me like that and walk away from me? Troy, you hear me! Troy! Troy!" she screams as I walk out of the front door.

By the time I got to my truck this little bitch came rushing me from behind hitting me in the back and the back of my head. The blow caught me off guard, causing me to stumble a little but when I got my composure I just react and grip that bitch around her neck.

"Honey, I'm tired of playing these f*cking games with you, now get the f*ck on before somebody gets seriously hurt...or worse! You know I can throw your little ass away to where nobody could find you, take my word on that. And the thing is, Honey, don't nobody give a damn about you enough to even come looking for you.

"Take that money and get on with your life, Honey. Consider this as a my gift from me to you," I threaten as I shove her petite little body to the ground, got in my truck and pulled off to get home to my beautiful wife and to rebuild my happy life.

Ravry Sloan

CHAPTER 12
Plans in Motion

HONEY...

Now where in the hell is this Splitz? I need to find that Nuki. She said she'd take care of me but what I really need is for her to help me take care of this damn Troy.

Oh, here it is. This shit looks cheap and funky as hell, damn! Pink Pussycats is at least a little bit classier than this ghetto hot mess.

"Damn, Lil Mama, what can I do you for?" asks this old fake ass pimp standing at the door as I walk up.

"No, I'm good. I'm just looking for Nuki."

"She's not here, yet. Does she know you're coming?" he adds sucking food from his crooked, stained teeth while looking me up and down like I was a piece of steak or something.

"No, I'm just a friend of hers."

"Hold on then, let me call her and see what time she's coming by today. Who are you anyway?" he asks as he strolls away to make his phone call.

"Tell her it's Honey," she'll know.

"So, you trying out?" inquires this long-legged, tall coco colored stripper coming in the front door.

"No." I answer nonchalantly looking around.

"Don't I know you?" she probes mean mugging me sideways.

"I don't know if you know me but I damn sho' know I don't know you."

"Ain't you a dancer?" she asks popping her gum.

"Yeah, I used to work at Pink Pussycat."

"Oh, that's where I know you from. I'm Juicy's cousin, you don't remember me from her birthday party, Twinkie?" she questions getting all up in my face as if I couldn't see her.

"Yeah, okay I remember now. Speaking of Juicy, have you talked to her? I've been looking for her and I really need to talk to her."

"You know what? Now that you mentioned it I haven't talked to Juicy in a while either. Her mom called me about a month ago telling me to let Juicy know that they just want to hear from her to make sure she's alright," she informs.

"Oh, wow! If you see or talk to her please tell her that Honey is looking for her, too!"

"I will, Girl. Why did you stop working at Pink Pussycats anyways?" she asks.

"Long story, but let me give you the thirty second version, *different shit, same smell*! The same ole' empty ass *Pretty Woman* effect that every other stripper dreams about, Girl. You know the one where a rich, handsome man will fall deeply in love with you and take care of you and you will live happily ever after for the rest of my life. For me it was really a bullshit nightmare," I describe as we both fell out laughing.

"Well, you know they are looking for dancers here, why don't you try out? You have a cute face and tight little body," she expresses as she smacks me on my ass.

"Good to know, thanks. I'll keep that in mind for future references."

"Nuki will be here in like 5," informs the fake pimp. "She said to wait right here and to not let you leave."

"Nuki? Oh, you're looking for Nuki? Oh, okay then," she rudely states walking off changing her mood to a straight bitch attitude.

"Don't pay her no never mind. That's just Twinkie, she thinks it is always about her, she all hard on the outside but all soft, white and gushy on the inside, she's harmless," says the fake pimp laughing at his own nasty joke.

"I don't pay these broads no never mind because they can't do nothing for me," I respond.

"But I bet Nuki can, she can get you paid. She has a way with the ladies and the ladies have a way with her, if you know what I mean?" voices the fake pimp while winking at me wearing a sinister grin.

"Ahhh, sweet, sweet, Honey, I knew you would come looking for me," greets Nuki as she walk in the door, tightly embracing me and kissing me on my neck. "Oh, excuse me I couldn't help myself," she giggles as she steps back to take me all in. "So what can I do you for?" she then asked taking my hand and leading me to the bar. "What you drinking?"

"Just a coke and add some extra cherries."

"So you're ready to climb on top of Big Nuki?" she asks while stroking my face with the back of her hand.

I couldn't quite reject her if I needed her so I now had to play along with this flirt game.

"Yeah, I've been thinking about you. Just wanted to know how you were doing and if you wanted to take me out sometime," I state throwing out some aggressiveness and allowing my finger to outline her neck.

81

"I said I wanted to take you out because I want to take you out but right about now you might as well tell me what you really want and get that out of the way. Come straight forward with Big Nuki, don't beat around the bush or try to charm your way to me. That's one thing Big Nuki won't tolerate. Never play me for a fool, understand?"

"Okay, here it is, I need your help getting back at somebody. I need this dude's life ruined. I promise I'll make it worth your while."

"What makes you think I'd be down for something like this?"

"Because I know you will, just call it woman's intuition," I say and laugh as I squeeze her hand.

"Let me guess, the person you want to get back at is that nigga, Troy Wilkins, who got you locked up, right?"

"Exactly! I only thought about you because I remember you saying your brother does *business* with him and I know exactly what that means. Besides, I don't want any of this to be connected to me. He will never suspect that we know each other and he won't be suspicious of anything what-so-ever."

"Okay, let me talk to my brother Mello and see what he can do to make things happen. My brother is his *business man* and Troy has been one of his loyal, longtime customers. What are you thinking about exactly? Setting him up with a rape or powder or something and having him sent to jail?" she asks.

"Mello? Oh, Mello is *your* brother? Me and Troy have been to a few *Private Affairs* at Mello's spot.

"But, no, I don't want him to go to jail or nothing like that I just want to embarrass him for embarrassing me. Now that I know Mello is your brother and just thinking about it I know anything that Mello hosts will be just the right atmosphere to bring that muthaf'cka down. I want to get him where it hurts. I want everything about this man questioned. I want him to be so embarrassed that he will want to climb under a rock, or hell, jump off of a ledge somewhere."

"So let me get this straight, you want this man's integrity and character exposed because you're mad?" she asks kinda making me feel stupid.

"Well, when you make it sound like that it does sounds bad but I'll be damned if he walks away from me and I don't get nothing. I've put in my work and my time and I deserve to be compensated for my committing to his foolishness and all of the bullshit I've had to endure."

"So how are you going to be compensated if the only thing that happens is that he is just a little embarrassed? What if it backfires? How is taking away what a man works so hard for going to benefit you and how is that payback?" she prods by giving me the third degree. "If he's broke, then you'll be broke, too, right?"

"That nigga got money and besides if his world is snatched out from up under him then he'll know exactly how I am feeling, and maybe then, he'd be willing to make sure I'm taken care of," I respond.

"It has taken me some years to get my dating service legitimate and to turn a very prosperous profit, but what I don't understand is how do you think you deserve anything if he worked as hard as I did? Did you not understand the rules of the game before messing around with a married man?

"I mean, shit, I've worked hard for mine and I'll be damned if I just let somebody take it away from me without a fight and I don't see a man like Troy Wilkins not fighting," she conveys. "Not with as much bank as he's holding."

"Well if nothing else, I think his wife should know he has a child on the way, because at the end of the day the baby is what all of this fight is about in the first place. It's not about me, it's about the baby," I try expressing with a straight face because I'm still not sure if I am actually pregnant.

"Well, I don't know how I can help but tell me what you want me to do?" she requests.

"Maybe you can get one of your girls to set him up at Mello's spot. You can get one of them to seduce him and have some pictures taken with him in an uncompromising position. Or I can simply just have his wife just show up so there won't be any questions about not seeing it herself. How does that sound?" I ask.

"It sounds like a woman scorned trying to get some payback, but hey, if that's what you want I'm sure I can make it happen."

"It sounds like that will work to me but whatever you do make sure she isn't one of these strippers because he can smell a cheap stripper a mile away. He wouldn't get caught up in that just because I'm sure he is kind of cautious right now.

"And whatever you do, please don't let him know that I have anything to do with this, at least not yet. Time will reveal who's behind the fall of Mr. Troy Wilkins in the end."

"Alright, if that's all you need me to do it's on."

"Okay! So you think you can really make this happen?"

"If this is all it takes to make you happy and for you to be my woman, yes," she states rubbing her hands up my thigh.

"See, I'm easy to please," I say not really wanting to laugh but can't hold it in anymore.

"I know I may sound childish but I cannot let this man just walk away and leave me penniless. II want him to be just as embarrassed as I am. I just want to shake his foundation a little and make him acknowledge and man up to his responsibilities."

"Well, I don't have an opinion about what happens to him, I'm just looking forward to what's going to happen between us," she specifies as she takes hold of my hand to lead me to an office at the end of the hall.

"I just got to have a taste of this sweet honey. Can I have some?" she asks as she overpoweringly kisses me, reaching her hand in between my legs.

"I just told you, I'm pregnant," I repeat not wanting to offend her before I get her to do what's needed to take care of Troy.

"What does that have to do with me? You make that statement like pregnant women can't have sex?" she updates, now freeing her hand away from me.

84

A Taste Of Honey   Ravry Sloan

"I'm just saying. I ain't never been pregnant before, I don't know the rules," I respond as we nervously snicker

"I'm not going to hurt you, now or ever! Trust me," she convinces and escorts me to sit on top of the antiquated desk.

"Here?" I ask.

"Why not?"

"Won't somebody walk in?

"Here, see…I will lock the door. Didn't I say trust me?"

Nuki walks over to me, lifts my little sun dress, opens my legs and leans against my breast. She holds me in a snuggly embrace for a few seconds then pulls back. The way she was staring through my eyes made me feel like she was trying to put a spell on me.

"You don't realize how special you really are, do you?" she questions.

She gently clenches the back of my neck, pulling me in to a seductive kiss. She began rubbing the outline of the opening to my private space with her fingertips. She lowly moans as her fingers slip slowly into my wetness, over and over again.

The rhythm of our bodies, the smoothness of her fingers massaging inside of me and the connection of our tongues sent electrical surges through my body. The music we were making was a love song.

Nuki drops down on her knees and rips my panties off to get to all of this sweetness. She places my feet on top of her shoulders, pulls me to the edge of the desk and puts her nose in me to briefly bask in the smell of me.

She takes both hands and exposes the pink and licks all of me. Up and down, down and up. Slow then fast, fast then slow; adding pressure with each of my excited whispers of pleasure,

She quickly teases my tip, continually, without a break or hesitation. Grabs hold around my thighs for resistance, keeping me from running away from the uncontrollably throbbing of my insides. I was powerfully squeezing and releasing my inner muscles over and over again with the momentum of her tongue flickering on my tip.

85

A Taste Of Honey   Ravry Sloan

My body normally tenses up, but not this time. My body keeps relaxing and falling victim to the release of pressure. I momentarily black out—lose all sense of hearing, seeing, control of limbs and speech—while I experience the most hardest orgasm i ever experienced.

And without any concern about who can hear us I let out a loud, long, sensual moan I release the hold! Nuki hurriedly stops with the teasing with her tongue and squeezes my tip with her two fingers as I cum, causing all of my juices to squirt across the room!

Damn, she is right I've never released like this before, let alone squirt! What in the world just happened to me?

"Oooh, there we go, I knew I was going to make you squirt! I like that. I told you when I first met you I could make you feel better than any nigga could. Now come taste how sweet I can make you taste," she orders standing up and leaning in for me to kiss her wet face.

Damn, she is right I've never released like this before, let alone squirt! What in the world just happened here?

Nuki wasn't a bad looking woman at all. Her skin was a flawless healthy complexion. She wore her hair in thick, long cornrows hanging down her back. She is confident in being who she is and that's what makes her sexy..

Or could it just be that I was horny as hell because I hadn't been with anybody since the last time me and Troy were together. It's been so much shit going on and I've been so distracted that I needed this as much as she wanted it I'm sure.

CHAPTER 13
Establishing the Rules

YODRA...

As much as I hate to admit it I am enjoying me and Troy getting close again. I really miss and think about Corbyn a lot, but I need for my focus to stay committed to what's truly important to me and that is my marriage.

I also recognize the main issue Troy has with me is me not wanting to satisfy his freaky appetite for sex. I was never overjoyed to participate in the games he always wanted me to play but this time I'm going to show him.

"Yodra, where are you?" yells Troy walking through the kitchen.

"I'm out here on the patio having coffee," I respond.

"Good morning, Baby," he greets with a kids as he sits down and pours himself a cup of coffee. "I had to run some errands this morning and I didn't want to disturb you."

"Good morning, Troy, and I understand. I really did want to sleep in today so, thank you" I inform.

"So listen, there is something I want to talk to you about. I want you to know that I really have been listening to you over these years," I reluctantly admit. "I love you enough to want to make you happy, as well as keep you satisfied since we are committed to restoring our marriage."

"Okay, Yodra?" he says with the look of suspicion on his face.

"Okay, here it is. What I'm trying to say is I'm willing to be your little freak," I express bashfully looking away with a shameful little grin on my face.

"My what?" he asks with a giggle and with eyes seeming to brighten up.

"Don't laugh, Troy. You always said that I wasn't aggressive enough for you in the bedroom and I didn't satisfy your freaky fantasies. Now, I'm willing to do whatever it takes to make sure you're satisfied," I state snickering right along with him.

"Yodra, I love you, Sweetheart. If for nothing else but the effort and the willingness to try," he expresses giving me a hug and lightly kissing me on the tip of my nose.

"I often think about what I would do differently if I was given another opportunity to work on my marriage and this is my conclusion. I will be more of a lover that you desire. Because of my own insecurities and selfish ways I denied you intimacy and satisfaction. I'm coming to you now to commit to being your freak!"

"Okay, but I'm not exactly sure what that means so why don't you tell me," he requests leaning back in his chair with his legs extended out with curiosity in his eyes.

"Well, I know how you've always fantasized about having someone join us in the bedroom, right?"

"Yeah," he hesitantly answers pulling his coffee cup away from his mouth.

"So, I'm willing to let someone join us in our bedroom, surprise!" I shout with my hands out stretched and my smile open wide!

"Really now?" he questioningly replies.

"You don't sound too surprised?" I ask mysteriously.

"Oh, no, I'm surprised! I just can't believe that you're initiating something like this."

"Now I'm feeling like a fool for even mentioning it, Troy. Damn!"

"Wait a minute. Calm down," he interjects. "I'm perfectly fine with it if you are. I just want you to understand how confident you have to be in the bedroom if you want this to work," he instructs.

"I do, but now I'm feeling a little bit silly for even bringing it up."

"Oh, no, don't feel silly, I'm flattered and excited but I think we need to talk about this a little more. Wouldn't you agree?" he asks.

"I agree. But, what should we talk about?" I interestedly ask.

"Like, who will choose the female?" he asks with a big grin.

"Who said it was going to be a female?" I question jokingly.

"Oh, oh, oh...I, I, I, just assumed..."

"I was just playing with you, Troy," I reveal.

"Okay, see productive dialogue already. We've established that it is going to definitely be a female. Now if I bring some woman home you're going to automatically think I already f'cked her so I'm going to let you be the chooser.

"It may be my fantasy but I truly need you to be as comfortable and open as possible. Yodra, Baby, I want you to enjoy this next level in our relationship, too!"

"I understand. I'm getting nervous just thinking about it now," I anxiously spoke.

"Is this a deep dark fantasy of yours, too?" he asks holding my hand and looking deeply into my eyes searching for the answers.

He thinks it's about him fulfilling his selfish fantasies and desires but honestly, it will give me the opportunity to have my freaky appetite fulfilled as well.

"No, Troy, a ménage a trios has never been a fantasy of mine," I answer going over in my head self-centered reasons to lie.

"Okay, so who f'ck's whom?" he ask eager to know the answer.

"I thought everybody did," I immaturely reply.

"As long as you don't have problems seeing me screw another woman in your face. And understand that this is just a part of the fantasy and not anything to disrespect you in any way," he assertively states.

"Okay, I understand that."

"So, when are we going to do this?" he enthusiastically asks.

Just thinking about it and seeing how excited I'm making Troy has me feeling very sexually stimulated.

"Why don't you let me surprise you," I inform as I get up and stand next to Troy.

I lift up my nightgown and sit across his lap, lying with my back on his chest. He delicately kisses the back of my neck and deliberately licks his way down my spine. My insides quiver as I grind on all of his hardness.

I demonstrate what my body needs by taking his hands, allowing them to outline my silhouette. I then purposely reroute his hands to gently message my breast.

I reach my hand in his basketball shorts to stroke his hardness. We seductively rub and kiss and grind and pant, filling our bodies with much energy and anticipation. I brush the stiff tip of his hardness along the outer lips in between my legs.

"You want me, Baby?" he asks as he suddenly inserts his hardness with a gentle force.

"Yes, Baby, yes!" I squeal as he bends me forward.

Troy holds me controllably around my waste, lifting me up until he slides right out of me. I grab his now glistening hardness and unhurriedly introduce him back inside of me, inch by inch. We both let out an exasperated sigh, releasing the build-up from the gratifying tease.

I didn't move, nor would I allow him to move. We passionately kiss as I squeeze tightly around all of his hardness. I tightly squeeze, and then release some; over and over again until neither one of us could take the buildup of internal compressions anymore.

Troy takes hold of the sides of my upper thighs and persuasively drives me down around him. I bounce harder and harder and harder and harder until in unison we release a high-pitch squeal. We lay there unmoved and unaffected while the housekeeper enters into the back patio through the side gate.

"Aaahhh, my morning coffee, thank you, Baby," he expresses as we both laugh like someone was tickling us.

"No, thank you, Baby," I remark. "I love my coffee strong and black topped off with a little cream," I tease with our bodies still intertwined within one another.

CHAPTER 14
The Private Party

TROY...

I can't help but think about the threesome I'm supposed to have with my wife. She is making me feel like the luckiest man in the world right now!

In the meantime I can still have a little fun, I boast looking at my reflection in the rearview mirror. I soon pull up to a *Private Party Affair* my boy Mello invited me to. I came just to blow off a little steam. I'm not even going to stay long. I promised Yodra I would come support her at an appearance at a community fundraising event.

Actually, this will be the first time I've ever come to this spot without Honey. What I wouldn't do for Yodra to experience this with me.

"Welcome Mr. Wilkins, will you be having your usual?" asks the beautiful, curvy cocktail server as I walk in the door.

"Yes, Hennessy straight."

"Mello asks that I escort you to his private room as soon as you arrive so follow me right this way, Mr. Wilkins," the server announce as she accompanies me to a private room downstairs. " I see you are you alone tonight," she notices.

"Yes, but I don't have to be," I reply looking at how sexy her ass is sashaying in front of me.

As many times as I've been to Mello's parties I've never been escorted to the *main room.* I wonder what makes me so special tonight I thought as I enter this huge red room full of seduction and sex.

Women with women, men with women, multiple coupling—moaning, groaning, smacking, crying, panting—I was witnessing sex at its best.

"Mr. Wilkins, welcome to the lap of luxury," articulates Mello as soon as I walk through the door.

"Thank you, but what do I owe the pleasure to be treated like a king and have access to the kingdom?" I ask inquisitively about the special treatment being offered to me tonight.

"Don't you think it's about time you've earned what goes on behind castle doors? This is the room for the king of kings," he says opening his arms as if to invite me to whatever was available in eyesight.

"But of course, but what did I do differently to expect this type of treatment," I inquire again.

"This is for being a loyal customer and this is your reward. You have been an active member going on two years strong and this is how we would like to show you our thanks for being such a devoted patron," explains Mello.

"Is this for real?" I ask again, but in a tone of delight and surprise.

"Yes, this is for real. No charge what so ever, but for this night only! By all means, enjoy yourself and get all you want and need," Mello informs.

A Taste Of Honey   Ravry Sloan

I observe the room filled with fine ass women of every race, height, and size looking to please me. All of the incentives are available to make anything happen tonight. Anything and everything I need in aiding in enlightenment of this whole experience is available--smoke, powder, alcohol and pills.

"Hello, Sexy, what can I do to please you?" ask this tall, blond vixen, taking my hand and slowly brushing it against her inner thigh.

"Do you like what you see?" then asks a spicy red head opening herself up so I could get a full view of her pink.

"Indeed I do," I respond as I watch them please each other. "You ladies look so damn good together," I praise.

"Thank you, Mr. Wilkins, our pleasure is your pleasure," states the red head.

"What can we do to please you?" ask the blond while putting her now wet fingers in my mouth. "Doesn't she taste good?"

I now know what she tastes like and all I could say is, "Damn, yes!"

In the blink of an eye the duo was unbuckling my belt and sliding my pants off.

"Damn, ya'll must really want some of this king sized dick?" I question as they both stroke and lick me up and down.

"Yes, Daddy," the blond positions when two more sexy ladies came to dribble on me, too!

The short one with the long ponytail leads my hand to her breast to message, and a little, tiny one takes my hand and inserts my fingers inside of her.

"Damn!" was again all I could say

The two lines I snorted and the alcohol must be really kicking in because I was loosening up a little more and began submitting to the seduction with a room full of freaks. I was really beginning to enjoy every minute of this orgy fest taking place on me.

"Troy, you need any help?" asks Mello as he was stroking himself and watching in excitement.

Even though I was in a good place sexually this whole scene was starting to get a little weird. I most definitely have to limit what I allow others see me do in public and this is where I am going to have to draw the line.

I assure Mello that I could handle it by myself. But he totally ignores my wishes. Suddenly he walks up to the tall blond, grabs her by her waist and powerfully forces himself inside of her. Rough and repeatedly, he dug deeper and deeper, harder and harder. I could see the pain on her now red face but she didn't stop him.

After he obviously finishes he slaps her across the mouth, drawing blood. He then spits on her as she balls up on the floor in pain and embarrassment. Another side of Mello appears that I never saw before and I knew that was my sign to leave.

"Now I'm paying you bitches to get me off all night long, so next!" he screams sprinkling a little cocaine on the head of his dick.

"Come and get it!" he then shouts like a mad man as the entire room broke off into a boisterous laughter.

He grabs this little bitty one, who was in the process of serving another guy, by her hair. He controls her down on her knees in front of him.

"Are you the bitch who asked for some lines? Well, here you go and you better not spit it out!" he orders as he violently burrowing deep into her mouth, holding her by the back of her head until she gags.

"And you better not throw up on this dick or I'm going to break your jaw!" he then threatens.

"Hey, Mello, chill out!" yells his boy Smooth. "There is *more* than enough for everybody. Calm down maaaan!"

"You're right, you're right the night is still young and I have plenty of time and there are plenty of bitches that can keep me *up* all night long," Mello proudly exclaims switching his mood entirely.

After watching that scene play out I knew I had to leave. I don't' want to get caught up in no rape shit. I felt as cheap and violated as that female must have felt.

Although this might have been a fantasy in my day the aggressiveness made me want to seriously dismiss myself from this atmosphere. All I want to do right now is to get out of here and get home to my beautiful wife.

"Why, Troy, you don't seem to be enjoying yourself anymore, is there something wrong? Is there anything I can do to relax you," Mello asks as I was finally able to escape the group's orgy fest and find the door.

"This is just not what I was expecting," I reply as I just want to just run out of here. "It is definitely time for me to go," I sternly reply, again, giving Mello a piercing stare.

"Awe, Maaan, you sure you can't stay? I have something very special in store just for you?" he informs as he literally smashes a pile of cocaine in his face. "This is your official initiation to this side of ecstasy."

"No, Mello, I'm good, thank you, but like I said I have really got to be going. This has been an experience I won't ever forget. I really enjoyed myself and I hope to return the favor to you soon."

"Are you sure? I really have something, or should I say someone amazing in store just for you. She is our prime choice and she will make you feel out of this world. Come on, Man, what do you say?

"And if you'd feel more comfortable you can go into one of the private rooms and you can have her all to yourself," he offers as he makes a hand motion toward the red curtain behind the bar.

"Speaking of the devil, here she is now," he states as we watch this sexy goddess glide over towards us, smelling like sweetness and looking like an angel.

"Troy, this is Jamaica and she is all yours," introduces Troy as he steps away.

Jamaica is a beautiful brown sister with hair hanging down to her perfectly shaped round ass. She has a tiny waist and thick

97

ass hips. It is definitely something sexy about her. The way she walks. The way the slightest touch of her hand on my chest had me standing at full attention.

She turns that big ass on me and steers my hand to squeeze her voluptuous, beautiful breasts. She takes hold of me by the back of my neck and services me to kiss her delicious smelling skin.

"Oh my, she wants you, Troy," laughs Mello as he encourages me to follow her to the private room off to the side of the main room.

"Jamaica, go grab my boy Troy another drink before you take him to heaven, or should I say hell!" instructs Mello as we stop in our tracks tip-toeing towards our escape.

"Thank you, Man, for changing my mind. This is definitely worth sticking around for," I express as I drool like a puppy following her with my eyes as she goes behind the bar. "I think I may need a few more lines before I dig into that," I lustfully convey to Mello, rapidly inhaling two more lines and throwing back the drink Jamaica handed me.

We finally head towards the private room and I think; now this is what I'm talking about! This is what I thought was supposed to happen down here.

"Knock yourself out, she's all yours," barks Mello as I quickly close the door, locking all others out.

No sooner than we enter the room something strange starts happening. After we start kissing and I begin feeling like a fog was engulfing the room and I became dizzy. It felt as if I were losing control. My body slowly starts to feel heavy, like I was becoming paralyzed, and my mind fades away as quickly as the darkness took over me.

CHAPTER 15
Never Satisfied

HONEY...

I heard about Onyx Trends Magazine hosting a fundraiser downtown at the Aquarium, so I decided to go down there. I felt like this is the perfect time for me to finally introduce myself to Mrs. Yodra Wilkins.

This should be interesting. The one thing I have always been confident about is being a freak to get a man. Obviously has something I don't have because she's able to keep the man, but little does she know I'm the bitch with the master plan!

I wonder how I will I react when I finally meet her? Will I tell her that I'm in love with her husband and I'm pregnant with his baby? We shall soon see.

"Hello. Hi. How you doing?" I repetitively spoke to the stuck up people as I made my way through the crowd.

A Taste Of Honey   Ravry Sloan

"Hello, have you signed up for any committees yet?" ask this frumpy older white lady holding a clipboard.

"Uuuhhh, no. I'm not interested but thank you," I respond without stopping for her to trick me into a conversation.

.   "How many children do you have?" ask another older sophisticated older woman walking up behind me.

"My husband and I just have the one girl," I lie trying to fit in.

"And what does your husband do?"

"Minds his business," I politely answer smiling pretty.

"I beg your pardon," she states with a look of shock on her face. "Robert, did you hear what she said to me? Robert?" she shouts to the guy standing next to her.

But before she finishes telling him the story I rush away to the other side of the room. I get a ginger ale so I would at least have something in my hand as I anxiously wait for Yodra Wilkins.

It is about damn time! She finally arrives and she was absolutely beautiful! She is what I would call classy.

She is wearing a simple, but elegant black dress, hugging her curves perfectly. There is nothing about this woman that looks cheap or ghetto to me.

"Isn't she just amazing?" proudly queries a group of ladies standing next to me admiring Yodra as she greets the people.

How can I compete with that? Look at how she can just command a room by just coming into it. And it's not because she's about to take off her clothes, either.

She stands with a perfect posture as she speaks with confidence to the supporters of her cause. I felt so low and out of my league now that I hate I even decided to come now.

I try desperately to try and escape quietly but in my effort to exit the room accidently I bump into the waiter. He drops the tray with the glasses of champagne, making a loud crash to the ground.

A silence fills the room in an instant and all eyes focus on us. I was so embarrassed that I run out to the bathroom hoping no one even notices me.

"Are you okay?" asks the voice on the other side of the bathroom stall door a few minutes later.

"Yeah, I just needed to make a quick exit," I embarrassingly reply.

"It's okay. Everybody has accidents and I'm sure the mess is all cleaned up by now, so come on back out here and continue having a good time joining in the festivities," politely states the unknown voice.

As I step out of the bathroom stall I was surprised to see that it is her, Troy's wife. "Oh, I apologize for ruining your party," I awkwardly say.

"As I said before there is no need to apologize, accidents happen and that's what the staff is here to do, so won't you please come back and join us?" she once more pleads. "At least stay around and let me by you a real drink at the bar when this is over,?" she urges.

For some reason I want to be in her presence so I agree. "Sure, I'll stay around."

"Good, it will be over in about thirty more minutes or so, so please don't leave. You promised, remember," she insists. "By the way, I'm Yodra Wilkins and you are?" she asks extending her hand.

She caught me off guard so I had to come up with a fake name, quick! I tell her the fastest name I can think of and can remember.

"My name is Sinclair Carter," I invent while shaking her hand.

My only real asset compared to hers is my willingness to be freaky with her husband. I'm the only one who accepted this no commitment shit and no f'cking respect in this relationship.

Now I'm pissed! I really feel cheap and used. Troy really has been using me for sex and never intended on being *my* man, that bastard!

We'll see how well she keeps it together when she finds out the truth about me and her husband. She may think she has it all but I guess it still wasn't enough to keep her husband home. I was truly just the other woman and that's the reason he pacified me.

"Are you ready?" Yodra asks after thanking all of her guest for their support.

"Sure, and this was a very nice event," I express.

"Thank you. It was a success. I feel good about it but now it's time to unwind and kick off my shoes."

"Was this your first event?" I asks being nosey.

"Since I have been fortunate enough to be truly blessed in so many areas of my life I always try to do something to give back.

"My next event is a young girls' self-esteem camp called *In the Pink*. The camp will empower and encourage girls to always believe in themselves, to always dream big and to never give up hope. But my passion project is a personal accomplishment, my art unveiling in a couple of weeks."

"Wow, congratulations! I wish there were programs like that when I was growing up and just maybe I would be have turned out to be a better person."

"Awe, don't say that. It's not that you would be a better person, say you would be a different person. I'm sure every decision you made in your lifetime you thought was a good and right decision at that time, right? So now is not the time to start regretting the decision already made, just learn to make different decisions from this point forward."

"Yeah, you're right it is time to make some changes in my life starting with my choices in relationships," I utter while constantly thinking about her husband.

"Girl, you better speak it!" she testify as we high-five one another and giggle.

"Well, thanks for the drink but I guess I have to be leaving," I announce after losing the nerve to say anything to her about Troy.

"Okay. It was nice…wait, I have an idea! Why don't we have a girls' spa day Saturday?" she asks with an excited look on her face.

"A girl's spa day? I don't know…" I hesitantly answer.

"Come on let's spend a day making up for our past decisions. Let's have our bodies and minds cleansed.

"I was just given these gift certificates for the Princess Pampering Package at Black Sands Spa. We might as well take advantage of them. Why not sooner than later?" she quizzes trying to convince me to agree to this outing.

"It will be nice, I promise. It states we will receive a full package—the full body message, a mud or sea salts bath, a facial or make-up art, and a mani/pedi," she reads the back of the certificate.

"This really sounds nice and relaxing. It also says that we will be served all you can drink mimosas and have access to the continental brunch buffet. Maybe afterwards we can go grab a real bite to eat, how does that sound?"

"Okay, you've convinced me, I'll be there," I finally agree.

"Okay, so the gift certificate states that we need to be there no later than 8:30 AM to get registered and checked-in, is that okay?," she asks handing me my certificate.

"Sounds good," I reply wondering what the hell am I doing.

"Great. Why don't you dial my number from your cell that way we'll have each other's number," she happily suggests.

"Oh, I don't have a cell phone," I reply humiliated because who doesn't have a cell phone?

"That's okay! Let me give you my number if anything comes up, that's how we'll solve that, okay?" she says handing me one of her business cards and leaning in to give me a hug. "It was so nice meeting you and I look forward to our girls' spa day.

As I walk away I couldn't help but think how charmed I was by her charisma, but not enough for me to spare her feelings about her husband. I don't have a choice I have to let her know about Troy and Saturday will be the day.

A Taste Of Honey   Ravry Sloan

This has absolutely nothing to do with her personally but everything to do with him and making his world crumble, shaking the core of his foundation. How I see it she really can't be mad with me. I'm not her husband and I'm not the one who owes her anything.

Troy is *her* husband and he's the one who owes her the commitment, loyalty and trust, not me. He's the one who is supposed to be faithful to her, not me. Why would he want to do this to a woman like this anyway?

Troy claims he is so miserable and unhappy at home, why not just leave then? I can't seem to understand why he wants to stay in such an

unhappy arrangement? Men...never satisfied.

CHAPTER 16

Finally... a Meeting of the Hearts

YODRA...

It's after two AM and I was really looking forward to Troy coming to support me tonight. He's been so loving and attentive these past couple of weeks but now I am wondering is he going back to the same old Troy. If I never can depend on Troy for anything it is to disappoint me. Mr. Unreliable, I was thinking when the doorbell interrupts my thoughts.

"Hello, Mrs. Wilkins, I'm Troy's friend Mello and I was just bringing him home."

"What happened to him? Is he okay?" I ask in a panic as he carries Troy's half-conscious body into the house.

"Yes, Ma'am, he just had a little too much to drink at the card game," he informs me after dropping Troy on the sofa then handing me his car keys.

He is in such a hurry to leave that he damn near runs me over as he tracks right back out the door.

"Okay, thank you," I angrily convey as I slam the door.

"Baby, I'm sick," is all Troy utters in between his moans as he lay sprawled out on the sofa.

"Well, I can see that! What in the hell were you drinking and why in the world would you drink so much anyway? And where have you really been that you couldn't come to my fund raiser?" I demand hailing a barrage of questions right at him. "And you better not get sick in this living room," I order now mad and with no concern about how he was feeling.

"Yodra, this is not the time for all of these questions. But I am sorry, Baby. I guess things just got a little out of hand and I lost track of time."

"I thought we were working on re-building our marriage, but this is the same old tired shit you always do, Troy. I'm not going to be the only one to put in the work."

"Yodra, I said I was sorry and I didn't plan on getting sick and I honestly didn't plan on missing your event, either. You think I really want to be sick and feel like this? I think I must have either eaten something bad or somebody put something in my drink."

"Oh, really, you think somebody put something in your drink? So where in the world were you, Troy, that you think somebody put something into your drink?" I ask in disbelief of both his and Mello's story.

"Like Mello said, hanging out with the fellas playing a few hands of cards."

"I guess I do not understand why somebody would want to put something in your drink or why you think this would even happen if you were simply at a card game with the *fellas*, Troy? It's just not making sense."

"I don't know, Yodra. I just started feeling dizzy and the next thing I knew I was waking up, so I must have blacked out. Look, Yodra, all I need right now is a little TLC not the third degree. I need you to help me and we can talk about this later when I'm feeling better, okay? That's what I need from my wife right now, to nurse me back to health, how about that?"

"Okay, Troy, you're right, I'm sorry. Tell me what you need me to do, what is that you want?

"Baby, I don't know! I'm sick and I need you to take care of me so figure it out, please, Baby," he expresses with sadness on his eyes.

"Okay, I'll start the shower and fix you some coffee. Do you think you can hold something on your stomach?"

"I don't know but I'll try, thank you, Baby," he whispers as begins throwing up on the floor.

"Ump, Troy, what in the world did you drink?" I ask in disgust while rubbing his back and trying not to throw up from the horrible putrid smell.

I actually felt sorry for him as he lay there moaning and groaning a little bit louder than before.

"Yodra, come on, please, not now. Please just help me, damn!" he shouts sounding aggravated this time.

I know Troy is still up to his old tricks. I don't believe one bit that he was at a card game this drunk hanging just out with the *fellas*. I know there had to be some women at this so-called card game, which would be the only explanation for someone putting something in his drink.

I just don't see a need or reason for guys to do something like that, sounds like some female characteristics type shit to me. Hell, he probably wasn't even at a damn card game just being honest about it. He was probably at the strip club.

What in the hell am I doing, I asked myself? Why am I so damn weak and gullible that I fell for this *working-on-our-marriage* shit? I was perfectly happy with the way things have been all of this time.

Corbyn just seemed to fill the voids that Troy always left empty and gave me the attention and affection I so desperately craved. What in the hell am I getting myself back into, I keep asking myself?

"Baby, are you going to help me to the shower?" he asks wiping the smelly drool off of his mouth.

"Yes, Troy, just lean on me, I got you," I say as we struggle getting up the stairs to the bathroom. I peel his sticky, vomit soaked clothes off as the wall help hold him up. "Can you get it from here?" I ask trying desperately hard to control my gags.

"Yeah, I think I can do everything else, thanks," he replies as he slums down to the floor of the oversized shower.

"Okay, I'm going back downstairs to clean up your mess and I will probably cook you a steak, some hash browns and some eggs."

"No eggs, hash browns and a steak will be just fine. Oh yeah, get me some coffee and make it black and strong."

"Okay, coming up," I answer like I was his short order cook.

I was really dreading going downstairs to clean up that stinking ass mess. I swear, why do I have to clean it up? Shit, he's the one who went out there and got drunk, not me.

I was going to surprise him and tell him tonight that I may have a candidate to join us in the bedroom, but forget it now. I've been excited all day to tell him that I was about to make his biggest sexual fantasy come true.

"Yodra," Troy bellows down stairs for me after getting out of the shower.

"Yes," I answer back.

"Are you finished yet?"

"Yes, I'm coming up now," I update serving him his order out on the balcony on the side of our bedroom. "Let's sit out here so you can get some fresh air," I suggest.

"Baby, I just want to say thank you for being here for me and for taking care of me. I truly apologize for missing your event.

How did it turn out?" he says searching for a reaction as he gazes into my eyes.

"It was successful, but I really wish you would have been there supporting me. It's lonely when I have to make up excuses for you and stand alone."

"I understand and I apologize for that, but there is nothing more I can do about tonight. I will promise that it won't happen again, okay, Baby?"

"I know but I thought we *both* were going to commit to working on our marriage, Troy?" I disappointingly say.

"Baby, we are. I didn't plan on things getting out of hand but you do have my full commitment I swear."

"Were there women at this card game, Troy, and be honest?" I ask knowing he wouldn't tell me the truth if there were.

"Come on, Yodra, I'm trying to really move past this but just so you'll know, no there were not any women there," he states as he put my feet on his lap to massage.

"You know you look stunningly beautiful to me right at this moment," he compliment trying to distract me from my curiosities.

"Thank you, but I just can't seem to put this to rest, Troy. Can you please help me understand why you think somebody would put something in your drink if you're really were hanging out with the fellas? This just doesn't make sense to me, Troy, this is something that woman would do," I reveal.

I was annoyed by now and I want answers, not apologies or instructions on what I should be doing to make him feel better.

"Why don't you make me feel better about all of this and just tell me what really happened?" I offer a little more room for the truth.

"Okay, Yodra, since you can't seem to let this go this is how tonight come about."

"Okay, thank you."

"Mello called me at the last minute inviting me to come by his spot to play a few hands of poker and to shoot a few games of pool to celebrate a the closing of a big business deal. All of the fellas and I took a few shots of Patron and then I had a few glasses of Hennessy.

"Mello had the night catered so I ate some of the food, which was Mexican. So between the alcohol and the Mexican food something made me so sick that I got dizzy and blacked out.

"There weren't any women there, just us guys. Mello drove me home and that was it and here we are still talking about it.

"For the last time I am so sorry for missing your event and for letting you down again, but this was the very last time, I promise. This will never happen again.

"Now can we please move past this and get *us* back on track, please? I'm really tired of talking about it and defending myself for some ideas you have swimming around in *your* head. Now, either you trust me or you don't," he explains looking me firmly in my eyes.

"Okay, Troy, I believe you and I'm done talking about it, too!" I cautiously reply.

I quietly try and gather my thought as we sit silently for a few minutes. I was admiring how handsome Troy was looking to me tonight as well.

"Troy, tell me something, what went wrong with us? Where did the harmony end and our separate lives begin?"

"When you started making me feel like you were rejecting me," he exposes.

"Rejected? I've never rejected you so you're going to have to do better than that, Troy."

"Every time I laid a hand on you, you pushed me away. I felt like my own wife didn't desire or want me anymore. I felt like I couldn't satisfy you anymore so I found somebody else who did."

"Troy, that's silly. I never rejected you and that's a sorry excuse for all of the messing around on me you've done. After Ivory-Jade was born you know I had to be there for her because I knew you wouldn't."

"That's not true, Yodra.'"

"Yes, it is, Troy! You could be a more hands on dad."

"You're totally missing my point, Yodra. I always understood about you taking care of Ivory-Jade, but it wasn't just that. You stopped making time for me. I didn't feel like I was a priority in your life anymore.

"Do you realize that you never touch me anymore? And that if I don't come on to you there is no action in the bedroom, or anywhere else for that matter? I feel like you lost the desire to care for my needs as your husband. You stopped making love to me and made me feel like it was duty. I felt so lonely and betrayed. I am your husband and I wanted you to desire me the way I desired you, and you didn't."

"Again, I ask, you think these are good enough reason for you having a baby on me and messing around with all of those different women for all of these years?" I ask not really trying to hear his poor attempt at finding an excuse.

"No, I'm not saying that those are good reasons but they are the reasons. This is the cold ugly truth and for that I'm truly sorry.

"Look, you asked what went wrong and I was man enough to tell you. Now, be woman enough to accept it. I love you, Yodra, I always have and I always will. And I want you to know that I never, ever stopped loving you. Are you willing to forgive me? And I mean completely forgive me for all of my past indiscretions?"

"I can and I will," I reply feeling guilty about my own secrets.

"Well, for me, Troy, things began going wrong when I started feeling like I was taking care of Ivory-Jade all by myself. I felt like I was the only one sacrificing in this marriage while you were out there doing whatever you wanted to do!

"I put my life on hold to be a mother to our daughter and you went out there and had a baby on me!

"I guess I felt rejected, too, because I didn't think you loved me anymore, either. I felt like there is no way you could really love me if you went out there and created another life with another woman.

111

"I expected that you would go out there and play around a little if I wasn't responding to you, but you stayed on the playground and never came back home.

"I felt like you owed me some ass kissing, especially since I accepted your legacy extending outside of our family, but you didn't. I was embarrassed and hurt so I built a world without you," I describe through my perspective.

"I guess we both had no idea that this is how each of us was feeling and that we are both responsible for making one another feel this way," Troy adds.

Baby, I am so sorry for making you feel rejected, that was not done intentionally. I think I neglected you because I was so angry about the baby instead of forgiving you completely. Can you ever forgive *me*?" I ask feeling humble looking in his eyes.

"I can, I will and I have. I just want my wife back and our marriage to be the way it is supposed to be. All I ever wanted is for us to be a happy family and I will be the most satisfied man in the world!"

"I agree," I respond moving from my seat to his lap, holding each other, feeling our hearts beats in sync.

"So where do we go from here? What's next," he asks after about ten minutes of being paralyzed in the moment of falling back in love again.

"The most important lesson we should have learned is to communicate our needs and forgive our past," I vow trying to cover my secret carelessness's without actually revealing any truths.

"Sounds like a plan to me! We'll start over from here mover forward," he agrees."

"And, by the way, Baby, I've always loved you and will always love you, too" I concur as we passionately kiss.

We walk inside to our bedroom, leaning within each other's body's creating an emotional love connection.

"I just want to hold my wife tonight and feel the intimate passion between us," Troy whispers in my ear as we doze off to sleep.

CHAPTER 17
That Night

TROY...

I feel a real sense of relief knowing that Yodra and I are finally starting over! I love my family and my life wouldn't be the same without them.

The only thing I need to do now is deal with this Mello shit. I don't know what in the hell is going on or what this shit is about, but I know I haven't been able to catch up to him since that night.

This is the day he normally plays basketball at the gym so I'm hoping this muthf'cka is here, I say out loud, quickly pulling in the parking spot right next to where he was standing with a small group of guys.

"Damn, what's up with you, Bruh?" he asks as I jump out of the car.

"What's up? You've got to be kidding me? That's what the hell I want to know. What in the hell happened the other night, *Bruh*?" I ask giving him a serious look as I slowly walk up on him.

"Maaan, I guess you just couldn't handle your liquor or you took too many lines or something. You were hanging with some real heavy hitters and it was some of that good powder. Not that normal dust you normally get from me," he explains dapping a few of the dudes still standing around us.

"F'ck that! Somebody put something in my drink, what gives, Mello?"

"Bruh, ain't nobody put nothing in your drink. Relax, just calm down. It was a wild night, and like I said, perhaps you took on more than you could handle. That beautiful wife of yours must be on that ass or something?" he questions as the fellas ooh and awe.

"Leave my wife out of this! You know what? You ain't even worth it," I calmly state seeing the crowd get bigger and security on the way.

"Generally, you would have to pay to play. And this is why those that can't afford to play don't. I bet it won't happen again," he laughs nudging elbows with the dude standing next to him.

"You know what, Mello, f'ck you!"

"That's all good, Bruh, next time," he whispers the closer he got by me as he walk to his car.

I was so pissed! What in the hell did he mean next time? I want to kick his ass, but what good would that do? I have an image to keep up so he wasn't worth it.

Besides, I would have had to explain all of this to Yodra. I guess sometimes you have to know when a battle is just not worth a fight. I'm going to have to just let that one go...for now.

"Are you leaving so soon?" asks this young, little, petite guy running up to me.

"Do I know you?" I probe with a puzzling look on my face.

He looks a little familiar but I can't place where I know him from.

114

"Troy, it's me, Omar," he advises with a big smile and excitement written across his face.

"Okaaay," I say still not having any idea who he is.

"From the private party the other night, remember?" he tries making me recall by hitting my arm, as if to say you know.

"Remember? You said that I could shadow you for a couple of sessions so I can learn correct workout techniques and you would help me create a workout routine to bulk up. Is today not a good day? Do you want to reschedule for another time?"

I really don't remember having this conversation with this guy, but if he says the *private party* then it might be true. Maybe that's why he looks like I've seen him before. Also, I truly need to pick his brain, if nothing more than to find out what he knows about *that night*.

"No, we're good just give me a minute. Go ahead inside and I'll meet up with you in a few," I finally reply.

"Okay, you really are a cool dude, Troy," expresses the young guy. "I didn't think that you were going to be a man of your word but you came through and that's what's up."

I appreciate his words of enlightenment and acknowledgment but unfortunately I can't seem to really remember him.

Even though I was full of tension and stress about that whole Mello situation, I still allow Omar to follow me during my work out.

"Did you enjoy the party the other night?" I ask opening up the dialogue.

"Did I? Yes I did! That was my first time going but the next time it will be for pleasure instead of work."

"Oh, what kind of work do you do?"

"I own a photography and video production company. Wait a minute...you don't remember me do you?" he asks in disbelief.

"Why would you ask me that?"

"Because, I am the one who was doing the filming. I'm not trying to tell you how to handle your business, Mr. Wilkins, but if

115

you can't handle this lifestyle you shouldn't be a part of it. Now if you don't mind, I'm leaving. Excuse me," he irritably answers, rolling his eyes at me and a big head twist.

I sat there lost as to what just happened! I must have said some things to that little guy under the influence of whatever I was on. I'll deal with that soon enough, I thought, stretching my body to relieve the stiffness.

I head to the massage area to help eliminate some of my stresses. I lay there on the table, as the heavy handed massage therapist kneads my tight muscles to loose. My mind eases as I drift off to sleep.

In my relax place a flash of Omar's face pops up in my memory.
I then remember seeing his face in the *private room* with me and Jamaica. My body jumps because I thought it was just the two of us in the room. I don't really remember too much after that.

I close my eyes and continue my solitary moment. I do everything I can to shake the images of Omar out of my head. Then another flash appears.

This time it is more detailed. I am getting pounded from the back by an unknown person while I'm giving head to Omar! I was looking up at him and that's why his face was familiar. What in the hell is going on? I thought ending my massage session?

"You aiiiight?" ask the masseuse.

"I'm okay," I uneasily express.

I quickly search to find Omar to now get some answers. I search everywhere but he must have left already. I even call Mello's phone but no luck.

I decide to go to take advantage of the sauna to try and clear my head before hitting the showers and going home to my beautiful wife. There were only two other men in the huge one room sauna and they seem immersed in their own seclusion.

I could feel my pores cleansing, as well as my mind. More bits and pieces of that night start to emerge.

A Taste Of Honey   Ravry Sloan

I remember going into that private room with Jamaica and at some point Omar was there. I don't remember him coming into the room, it's like he was just there.

What in the world did I do? There is something shady about that night and I need to get to the bottom of it.

For the first time in all of my indiscretions I am beginning to panic. I've always had control over what I was doing, right or wrong, but that night something took control over me. I can't prove it but I know deep down in my gut that something was put in my drink. My mind was altered, forcing me not to remember *that night* or my actions.

A Taste Of Honey

Ravry Sloan

CHAPTER 18
Breaking the Silence

HONEY...

After checking my e-mails on CeeCee's laptop, I see Mello still has not sent me the proof. It's been about a week. I wonder what's taking so damn long.

Thankfully the opportunity presented itself in a strange way and I just can't wait anymore. His wife seems to be nice enough but since Troy didn't spare my feelings why should I spare hers? There is definitely going to be a change of plans…today!

"Where are you headed so early on this nice Saturday morning?" CeeCee asks as I just finished getting dressed.

"I have a girls' day scheduled with a new friend. Take a guess and see if you can figure out who it is?" I request intriguingly.

"Uh oh, who is it, Honey?" she remarks rolling her eyes.

"What would you say if I told you Troy's wife?" I reveal feeling a bit of relief after holding that secret in all week.

"What…with his wife?" she examines looking predictably in shock.

"Yes, can you believe it? Her name is Yodra Wilkins and I met her at an event last week. We actually sat down and talked a little bit over drinks. She *is* gorgeous and super nice. Too bad I'm going to have to destroy her world by telling her about her no good husband," I state now including CeeCee in my plans.

"Honey, I'm speechless! I don't even know what to say. Why are you so determined on destroying their lives just because things didn't work out for you?"

"I don't need your judgments right now, CeeCee. I've made up my mind and he will not get away with playing with my emotions and destroying my life. Payback is a bitch and I'm the bitch doing the payback. I'm waiting on the proof right now, you just mark my words, I will destroy him!"

"Wow! And you think this will give you the satisfaction you need to compensate for what you did wrong? You knew you were wrong messing around with a married man. Why destroy them because of your weaknesses?"

"Because, of the baby. You just don't understand, CeeCee."

"A baby you may or may not even be carrying."

"Well I could be."

"You should put first things first. For real, you need to find out if you are pregnant. And if you are, how are you going to raise it?"

"With Troy's money, that's how. I was doing me and he came chasing after me. So while you're trying to make me feel bad about messing around with him, *he* was the one who was married with the obligation and he knew that, too!"

"Okay, sounds like you've got your mind made up about this and you're not trying to see it from any other way accept your way."

"I'm sick of going back and forth with you over this subject so thank you for letting me live my life my way. Even if it's not how you see fit. You act like you have never made a mistake or fell in love with the wrong person, so don't judge me!"

"Alright, I hope you can sleep at night and can look at yourself in the mirror because you're the only one who has to live with you and the decisions you make," she preaches.

"I really don't get you, CeeCee. I know you're somewhat of a-goodie-two-shoes but it seems like you don't want me to get what's due to me.

"And why do you keep referring to me and Troy's situation as *them*? I'm not trying to destroy *them*; I'm going to destroy *him*. He's doing that to her all on his own.

"This has me kinda confused about your loyalty to our friendship, CeeCee. Why does this matter so much to you anyway? It's not like it's affecting you so what gives?"

"You mean you really don't know after all of these years? If it involves you then it involves me and that's all I have to say about that. I guess I seem to care more about you than you do…I guess."

"CeeCee, you know I love you and I appreciate all of the love and concern that you have for me but I'm just angry and confused right now. I really don't know what I *need* to do but what I feel I *must* do you keep on beating me over the head about it.

"You may not agree with my way but all I'm asking is that you respect that it is my way. It's not about you and I'm sorry if it affects you, but this is about me and my life. Just be my friend unconditionally that's all I need for you to do right now," I plead.

"So if you feel so strongly about telling his wife about you and Troy, why didn't you just tell her the other night when you met her?"

"I was, but she was so friendly and personable I lost my nerve."

"Don't you think it would have been easier when you didn't know her than it will be now? She may feel bamboozled don't you think?"

"Well, I guess we'll find out soon enough, huh? Wouldn't you want to know if your lover or spouse was cheating on you for years *and* maybe having a baby?"

"Well, like you said, you weren't worried about poor little wifey's feelings when you were screwing him and reaping all of the benefits you received," she adds mockingly.

I slap CeeCee's face and run out of the door. Maybe CeeCee is right, this is too much to try and understand.

I knew she was going to throw a guilt trip on me. I figured since I was going to ask her for a ride I knew I was going to have to tell her where I was going.

As I stood at the red light waiting to cross the intersection this little light blue BMW starts blowing at me.

"Hey, you want a ride?" screams Twinkie, the stripper from Splitz.

"Girl, yes, thanks. I am in desperate need for a ride," I reply.

"Where are you headed?" she asks.

"To The Black Sands Spa in Buckhead."

"Oh, cute place so I hear. I've been meaning to go and check them out for a while now. By the way, I finally found out where Juicy has been for the past 6 months," she informs, turning down the radio.

"Where?" I ask nosily

"Juicy has been strung out on drugs so bad that she's has been out there prostituting just to get a high. She been back and forth in and out of jail and rehab centers," she advises.

"Whaaat, not Juicy? I'm a little surprised at that because she didn't seem like the type to get on heavy drugs like that."

"Yeah, I agree. Her mom told me that whatever drugs she's been on have caused her to somewhat lose her mind. She has severe memory loss that she can't even remember her name or really even care for herself at times.

"I'm telling you Juicy is in real bad shape. She's now living with her mom and her mom is already taking care of her son. But my aunt says she doesn't think Juicy will ever be right again," she states sounding sad.

Juicy has a son? I didn't know Juicy had any kids, I thought.

"Wow! I'm so sorry to hear that. I didn't even know Juicy had any kids?"

"Yeah, this is her only child, little Joshua. He was born with Down's syndrome and requires a lot of attention. But, the good thing that came out of this is my aunt is financially secure. Whoever Joshua's dad is makes sure he has the best medical care possible and my aunt is never lacking for anything," Twinkie divulges.

"Who is her baby's daddy?" I curiously ask, hoping she was going to say it is Troy's baby.

"I don't know but I heard he was of her frequent customers from the club. And he has a *whole* bunch of money. Like I said, this is just rumor I don't really know. Her mom says that he never comes to see Josh, but hell, neither did Juicy," she exposes with a loud laugh.

"That's messed up," I comment trying to shake the strong feeling thatTroy is Juicy's baby's daddy.

"I just may go by there to see her and I'll tell her you asked about her," she offers as I get out of her car..

"Okay and thank you for the ride."

CHAPTER 19

The Courage of Tiny Bubbles

YODRA...

I'm going to do this! I don't care how nervous I am, I am going to do this, I thought. I am trying to convince myself that this is the right thing to do for my husband and our marriage.

I'm scared to death of what her reaction may be but I'll never know unless I ask. What if she gets angry, slaps my face and storms out? What if she says yes? I've run these scenarios over in my head a thousand times and I'm still not quite sure how I am going to approach her.

"Sinclair, I'm over here!" I shout when I see her walk into the earth toned colored, granite lobby of the spa.

"Hey, how are you?" she asks as we double kiss each other on the cheeks.

"Hey, Girlie, I'm well how, are you?"

"I thought I wasn't going to be able to make it. I almost didn't have a ride," she tells.

"Well, you're here now and that what counts. Are you ready for a day you'll never forget?" I request, secretly having more than one meaning behind my statement.

I reach in my purse to turn my cell phone on vibrate when I saw I missed two calls from Corbyn. I was excited when I saw that it was her, but her timing was bad.

"Damn," is all I could say.

"Is everything okay?" asks Sinclair, looking a bit more nervous as I was.

"Yes, everything is just fine. I'm looking forward to a day of relaxation and fun," I say as the calming, ocean sounds of the music began filling the room.

"I've never had services done at a full spa before," she inform me as we walk into the locker room.

We undress and put our clothes in the locker. I take a peek at Sinclair's body as we wrap ourselves in the plush, lavender bath robes. I thought, Troy may find her sexy.

"Good morning, Ladies, my name is Andres and I'll be your personal attendant for the day. What would you ladies like to start off your morning?" he ask with his thick Spanish accent.

"Today feels like it's going to be one of those days to escape into solitude so I'm starting off with a nice bubbly mimosa."

"I'll have the same," stated Sinclair.

"Coming right up, Ladies, and please don't hesitate to help yourselves to the self-serve buffet just around the corner or if you'd like, I'm available to get anything you may need or want as well.

"Thank you," we both said in unison.

"This is so nice," I exclaim admiring the ambiance.

The beautiful photography artwork makes me curious as to what Corbyn wanted. We haven't talked since we met at the coffee shop.   "It really is and I feel like I'm a superstar," she replies as we toast our champagne flutes and sip on our fresh cold mimosas.

After getting the long list of logistics out of the way we start letting our guards down and begin enjoying each other's company.   I notice our flirting intensifies around the second mimosas.

She touches my arm lightly when we laugh and I reciprocate and caressing her leg.   We constantly lean on one another as if we just can't hold ourselves up without help from the other.   We grab hands frequently as we talk.

Our bodies were always, at some point, in contact whether it be our hands, or arms, or legs, or shoulders.   I begin falling weak to the tiny bubbles that are taking over my desires.   As we lay back relaxing in the hot tub I slowly ease into the proposal.

"So, Sinclair, you seem to know a lot about me but I don't know much about you."

"So, what is it you want to know?" she ask looking as relaxed and loosened up from the massage as I was

She stares into my eyes and rubs the back of her hand along my cheek.

"Are you married? Do you have children?" I ask.

"No, I'm not married, but I hope to be some day. As for kids, well let's just say I'm working on it," she answers and falls into a boisterous laugh.

"You know you never really told me what you do exactly. I know you said that you were in entertainment but what do you do in entertainment?"

"Well, since we're being so honest with one another and you've been so nice I might as well tell you the truth. I'm an out of work stripper, but please don't judge me."

"Why would I judge you? A job is a job, right?"

"Yeah, but you seem so educated and worldly that I thought maybe you would look down on me if I told you what I actually did. Let me tell you why I say I'm an out of work stripper," she states my cell phone ringing from my robe pocket interrupting us.

127

"I thought I put my phone on vibrate. I apologize for that. Let me see who it is," I instruct.

I get out of the water to check who was calling and it was Corbyn again. What is going on? Should I answer?

I'm going to have to ignore her call for now and just call her back later. I'm trying to stay with the momentum and the mood to finally ask Sinclair the big question.

"I'm sorry about that, that was one of my friends but I can call her back later. Would you like to get another mimosa?" I question, changing the subject.

"Sure, might as well."

After our fourth mimosas were brought to us we were just about ready for anything.

"Now, would you mind if I ask you a few personal questions?" I inquire trying to feel her out.

"Go ahead, I'm an open book," she offers.

"When you were a stripper did you ever sleep with any of your customers?"

"Occasionally, but they really don't like for us to that so I had to do it on the down low."

"Were any of your customers women?" I nervously investigate, hoping she won't slap me across my face.

She looks intently at me for a second with a stone face.

"Yes, couples actually. You'd be surprised at the couples who often frequent strip clubs looking to spice up their sex life. Or the woman that want to learn a few tricks to take home to satisfy their man."

"Did I offend you?" I consider not sure if I should continue after the few moments of silence.

"No, you didn't offend me because most people think that strip clubs are for horny, perverted men. Let me tell you they should be the classroom for sex, how to be sexy, how to please each other with sex, and how to heighten your sexual pleasure," she reveals.

"You'd be surprised at how many *married* men come to strip clubs because they are not being satisfied at home and we become their fantasy. So let me tell you…"

"Wait, wait speaking of a fantasy, I really want to ask you something very, very personal. I am so nervous and embarrassed and if you want to slap my face or walk away after I ask I'll completely understand."

"But I need to say something to you," she states with a serious look.

But what I have to say was on the tip of my tongue now and I need to just spit it out while I still had the nerve.

"Sinclair, look, I really have enjoyed your company today and I think you are a beautiful sexy woman. I've been feeling some attraction to you over the course of the day and now I'm feeling a certain kind of way toward you. How does that make you feel?" I finally unveil, rubbing the back of her hand and feeling a slight bit sexually aroused.

"Whaaat?" she queries with my statement totally catching her off guard.

"I find that I am very attracted to you and I think you are very sexy, and I'm sure my husband would find you just as attractive. So I would like to know if you would please join me and my husband intimately in our bedroom to fulfill our sexual fantasy." I propose in disbelief that the words finally came out of my mouth.

We both just sat there in silence, gawking into each other's eyes as I start thinking that this is the calm before the storm.

"Let me get this straight, you want me to join you and your husband intimately to fulfill your sexual fantasy?" she repeats the proposal.

"Yes," I answer, looking away feeling ashamed and embarrassed that I must have insulted her.

It seems like we are sitting for minutes but in actuality it was just a few seconds.

"Yes, I'll do it!" she responds with a big ass grin on her face.

"You will? You will!" I shout.

We scream as we embrace our naked, wet bodies together. She then leans in and give me the most sensual, softest kiss. Just slightly touching my lips with hers, but that small little gesture turns my sex on high and I began to throb intently.

"So when will this little fantasy take place?" she questions, holding my hand sitting motionlessly from the unusual requests.

"I want to do it as soon as possible. I want this to be a surprise for my husband so we will just have to plan a date."

"Why don't we do it this evening," she suggests. "But let it still be a surprise. You bring me home with you and together we walk in the door, now that will be the real surprise."

"You think? Okay, I'm with it." I answer reluctantly but feeling all giddy inside.

"I need to call to make sure he will be home," I inform her.

I, again, get out of the hot, comforting water to call Troy.

"Hello, Troy," I enthusiastically greet.

"Hey, Baby, it's so good to hear your voice. You've been gone all day, I've been missing you," he replies so sweetly.

"Hey, Baby, I was just making sure you were home. I was going to grab us a bite to eat and I want to see what you want?"

"Where are you going?" he asks.

"Umm, I don't know yet."

"Well, why don't you just surprise me? And don't forget to bring me home something sweet to eat," he insists.

"Oh, I will absolutely bring you something home very tasty and satisfying. You will definitely be surprised," I discretely imply as I felt my insides tremble with nervousness and excitement.

CHAPTER 20

Dots Connected

TROY...YODRA...HONEY...

I really want to show Yodra I am breathing life back into our marriage. I want this weekend to be special since her art unveiling and Ivory-Jade will be home next week.

I put the candles starting at the door winding around to the patio. Rose petals sprinkled on the path and some jazz in the background. I chill her favorite bottle of Chardonnay, and then take one last look confident that this should definitely do it.

I was on my second glass of wine when I heard the garage door open. Then I heard two car doors slam, thinking two car doors? I got up to help her with the bags, but before I get to her, she was already in the house.

"Baby, I'm home and I have a surprise for you, but stay where you are," yells Yodra after coming in. "Oh, look how sexy the house looks.   All of this just for me?" she comments enthusiastically.

"I'm right out here on the patio, Baby, and yes this is all for you. You like it?" he asks devotedly.

"I mean it, stay right there! I have to tell you something," she instructs again.

"I hope you brought something good for me to eat. I'm hungry as hell," he eagerly replies, rubbing his hands together and licking his lips.

"Baaaybeee, I like the house! This is so thoughtful, thank you," she genuinely acknowledges.

Yodra wraps her arms around Troy, giving him a deep passionate kiss.

"Okay, here is the surprise. Do you remember when we were talking the other day about us participating in a ménage trio?" Yodra gingerly reminds Troy.

She tenderly kisses him softly on his neck and runs her fingers tips across his exposed chest. Hoping to persuade and entice him into saying yes.

"Yes, Yodra, what's going on?" he asks, feeling the swelling inside his white silk lounging pants get bigger with every touch.

"Just the thought of having a threesome turns me on," Troy jokes hunching up on Yodra's butt.

"So, get ready?" Yodra surprisingly initiates, leading him by the hand.

"I am!" Troy excitedly replies, following her in the house to what was waiting.

"Baby, this is Sinclair Carter and she is the sexy woman who has agreed to join us tonight. Surprise!" shouts Yodra.

"Hi, Troy, it's so nice to meet you," expresses Honey like they just met.

Honey walks up to Troy, extending her hand to introduce herself as Sinclair. She takes advantage of her back being to Yodra and looks Troy sternly in his eyes and winks.

Troy stands there, paralyzed with fear and confusion.

132

"Yodra, what in the hell is this? What in the hell is going on here?" he interrogates, looking like he just saw a ghost.

Are these bitches trying to set me up, Troy thought?

"Troy, are you not surprised? I met her last weekend at the fundraiser event. You know the one you missed. I've spent the day getting to know her at the spa and over a little retail therapy. I find her physically attractive, don't you?" Yodra presses a response from Troy, feeling like a winner,

"Yodra, let me speak to you in private, please?" Troy asks, aggressively directing her to the patio.

"Yodra, what in the hell is going on and who is this woman?" he demands, talking in between his teeth.

Maintain my demeanor and keep it together, the voices in Troy's head keeps saying.

"I think she is ideal for us. She's beautiful and she has experience being with a couple. Don't you find her attractive, Baby?" she again asks showing obvious signs to Troy's resistance.

"Sinclair Carter? How do you even know that is her real name? How are you going to just bring a stranger up in our house to sleep with us? I didn't expect you to bring somebody *home* to do this, Yodra. What if she is a psycho killer or something?" he stresses.

"Did I do something wrong, Troy? Do you know her or something?" Yodra grills, now not feeling the excitement from Troy.

"No, no, no, that's not it at all, you did well, Babe. I am taken off guard. You're fine. It's okay," Troy states reassuring Yodra and not causing further doubt.

"Okay, so let's go back into the house. I think it was kind of rude that we just left her standing there. So this is definitely going to happen tonight?" Yodra inquires, draping her arms around Troy's neck with enthusiasm.

"Yes, Baby," Troy answers, going back in the house and runs immediately up stairs.

Out of all of the ladies in the world to bring home, how in the hell did Yodra find Honey's psycho ass? This sounds like

133

some real stalker type shit Honey already had planned, Troy thought.

"Okay, Sinclair, I apologize for that but we are in a mutual agreement. I'm going to go upstairs and put on one of my new sexy outfits. Just give us a few more minutes and I guess we'll get started.

"Sounds good," Honey replies.

"Is there anything you need?" Yodra asks Honey.

"Just your bathroom," Honey requests with confidence growing on the inside.

"By the way, you can help yourself to anything you'd like off the bar," offers Yodra, showing Honey to the downstairs bathroom.

Honey, says to herself in the mirror, I am one lucky duck. I can't believe this is actually about to go down. I can't wait to make this muthaf'cking Troy squirm.

This muthaf'cka round here acting like the faithful husband in love and sexing up the house and shit, I angrily think until something on the wall distracts my thoughts.

Wait a minute…is this a CeeCee Carter original photograph hanging behind the bar? How is it that they have one of her most famous photographs in their house? Either this is an unimaginable coincidence or they must know one another.

That's strange, CeeCee never mentioned knowing Troy when I told her about him a couple of weeks. Nor did she mention knowing Yodra earlier today, either. This may explain why she's been acting a little holier than thou. She knows them and want to protect them.

This all could be just a fluke since Troy and Yodra are such patrons of the arts. Maybe, just maybe they happen to like her work and bought it from one of those galleries or showings. Perhaps I'm putting too much into things, but I do know CeeCee is real fond of this piece. I wonder what gives.

Honey feels no concerns about the possibility of a pregnancy, after throwing back a couple of shots of Patron. She walks around admiring the beauty and size of their home.

134

I hope to have this with Troy and our child real soon, Honey whispers.

Yodra's cell phone has been blowing up all day, so being nosey Honey looks on the screen. And to her surprise *Corbyn Carter's* name appears.

What in the hell is going on? Why is CeeCee calling Yodra? How in the hell do they know…but before finishing her thought, Yodra's phone rings again and again.

What is CeeCee up to, Honey quizzes?

"Sinclair, are you okay?" yells Yodra from the top of the stairs startling Honey from her nosiness.

"Yeah, I'm good and relaxed," shouts Honey.

"Sorry for the wait," Yodra states frolicking gracefully down the stairs.

"You look amazing!" Honey states adorning Yodra's beautiful figure in the racy lingerie.

"Thank you," Yodra shyly responds.

"Come here, Sexy. I poured you a shot of Patron. I knew you would be a little nervous and this should help you relax."

"Thank you. And yes, I am very nervous," she replies taking two quick shots.

"Here, take another one. I promise this will be the one to knock the edge off," Honey informs, now lusting for some physical stimulation from Yodra.

"Yeah, I'm definitely feeling it," Yodra utters.

"Can I touch you?" Honey asks, unable to fight the temptation of feeling frisky from the shots.

"Sure, come on," she says allowing Honey to feel the form of her figure.

"You smell so damn good, umm," Honey softly compliments in Yodra's ear, their cheeks lightly brush against one another.

Where in the world have I smelled that fragrance before, Honey wonders?

"What is that delicious fragrance you have on?" Honey curiously asks after finally recognizing the scent.

"It's called Rain Shadows, a very expensive fragrance from Africa. It comes from a rare flower in the foot hill of the mighty Congo," she proudly explains, seeming eager to discretely tell her secret.

Is this the woman CeeCee has been seeing and can't seem to talk about because it's so *complicated*! Well I'll be damned! The little misses isn't so sweet and innocent after all.

I finally connect the dots! The CeeCee Carter original photograph hanging on the wall behind the bar, the consistent phone calls today from Corbyn and now this rare perfume that CeeCee says her *sweetie* risks to give to her as a gift.

I may not have a college degree, but I am smart enough to figure this thing out. My lesbian ex-girlfriend, and best friend, is messing around with my lover's wife, what in the hell?!

CHAPTER 21
And the Winner Is...?

TROY...YODRA...HONEY...

I pace the room furiously, trying to think of a way to get out of this messy situation. I'm trying my best to avoid Yodra's womanly sixth sense radar picking up on anything out of the ordinary.

How in the hell can I go through with this knowing Honey is trying to destroy me? My marriage will definitely be over if it ever comes out about me and Honey. This is more than just cheating; this is the ultimate form of betrayal.

"Troy, what's taking so long, Baby?" calls Yodra from downstairs.

Okay, I have to think fast. I have an idea. I'll just have to figure out a way to be in control at all times, Troy constructs.

A Taste Of Honey   Ravry Sloan

"Since we are waiting on your husband to come down stairs, can I have a kiss? I can't wait any longer to see how scrumptious you taste," Honey makes her feelings known, uncovering her erotic side.

"Sure," Yodra replies, placing her hand on the back of her neck and pulling her in for a kiss.

"I know. So you can go ahead and let go," says Honey, gently taking hold under Yodra's chin.

"What does that mean?" Yodra asks, slowly pulling away from Honey to read the meaning in her eyes.

"Come here, Girl!" Honey insists by hugging and seductively pecking down her neck.

Yodra's body soon gives in, becoming powerless to the struggle to resist. Their bodies move in unison like a choreographed dance.

A surprised Troy enters the room, shocked to see his that Yodra and Honey already started. Troy stands there in silence, watching the foreplay unfold. Envy builds up within him as his looks turn to anger.

Yodra is being pleased by my lover, Troy accepts. He watches Yodra's body tremble, craving more of Honey's touches. After standing there for a few minutes, his hands begin to wander down to his stiffness.

Honey sees him satisfying himself and gives him a thirsty eye and winks, again. He wants to go over and unlock their intertwined bodies and choke the shit out of Honey, but how can he without causing Yodra to be suspicious?

"You ready to join us now, Troy?" Honey asks in the midst of kissing Yodra's neck.

"Come on, Baby! Isn't this what you've been wanting?" Yodra retells me of my fantasy.

He could feel the heat from across the room and smell the sex drifting in the air. Troy releases the resistance to hold on to his anger and accept the passion that was overwhelming his dick.

Troy lusts while Yodra and Honey's bodies grind in tempo. Their tongues wrestle every time their mouths aggressively connect.

Troy walks closer to the ladies, pulling Yodra by her hair at the back of her head. This forces her to turn her face in his direction, following with a seductive kiss. His other hand finds its way to her naked breast.

Purposely being attentive and passionate to Yodra, Troy totally ignores and dismisses Honey as if she wasn't even there.

"Do you want to kiss her, too?" Yodra asks rotating her attention to Troy.

"No, I want you two to continue enjoying and playing with each other, I'm enjoying the show," he replies making sure to not give Honey the satisfaction of touching him.

"You can, Baby, I won't get mad," Yodra instructs.

"It's no fun if we all can't join in," Honey chimes in allowing her hands to touch Troy's naked chest.

"I have no desire to be intimate with you what-so-ever," he skillfully answers trying to gain control, noticing the blood boil up in Honey's now red face. "My only wish is to see you please my wife."

"Are you sure?" Yodra asks innocently. "There are no rules tonight, whatever you want to do is allowed, Baby. This is your night, your fantasy coming true," she educates while taking Troy's hand and positioning his fingers inside of her as Honey's hand follows.

Yodra's body was in perfect sync with the rhythm of their hands satisfying her body, making her insides throb with ecstasy. Making harmonizing love sounds in between the tantalizing kisses from Troy sandwiching her from behind and Honey's mouth playing with her nipples in front.

"Are you enjoying this?" asks Honey, trying to join in on Troy's kisses, but quickly he pulls away and begins lightly nibbling on Yodra's ear.

"Oh, yes, Sinclair, yes I am. How about you, Baby, are you enjoying yourself?" Yodra asks Troy opening her eyes for the first time since the three-way game of seduction began.

"I'm enjoying watching you enjoy yourself, Baby. You look so damn sexy and you sound so good," he softly utters in her ear as he massages his hardness along her thigh.

The pace of Yodra's body and their hands sped up as the love sounds got louder. Yodra and Honey kiss a little deeper, more dramatic. Troy tickling her neck with his tongue, moving back up to her ear t.

Yodra being the recipient of unselfish gratification exhibits her satisfaction by releasing sudden sequences tightening up around their fingers. Pleasure cries fill the room. With sudden intensity her erotic flow overflows as she lets out a loud love call. Troy and Honey feel the explosion erupt on their fingers as Yodra's erotic juices ooze down her thigh.

"Yeah, that's it!. Now, can I have some of this?" Honey expresses, slowly squatting down in between her legs. She proceeds to lick the juices from her inner thigh.

"Can she taste you, Baby?" Troy asks with eager anticipation of seeing his wife's body squirm and wiggle with enjoyment.

"Yes, Baby, are you going to join us?" Yodra inquires as she strokes Troy's hardness along her outer lips.

"I may," Troy answers with a little less enthusiasm than Yodra expects.

Troy watches Honey climb on top of his wife…Seeing their bodies move together like the waves in the ocean. They bump clits, desperately reaching for a penetration-less climax. And then in a slow motion grind, they both cry out like a band.

Without missing a beat, Honey slowly eases her way to kissing Yodra's neck, moving at a snail's pace down to her breast. Being patient with both nipples, and then down the path to her bellybutton.

Honey kneels down effortlessly between Yodra's legs, spreading her open to expose her pink. She begins taking pleasure in tasting her from the back to the front, stopping only to tickle her head. Front to back, back to front, over and over again, easy then fast, fast then easy.

The expressions of contentment and bliss on Yodra's face convey she can't take it anymore. Troy decides that he's had enough of being left out and he is ready to satisfy his wife and take control back of this whole situation.

With adrenaline flowing from other selfish intentions Troy's manhood begins growing even harder and his desire grows stronger.

"Baby, come here," he aggressively requests and tugs Yodra's away from Honey, guiding her curvaceous body to sit on top of his erectness.

Honey realizes she just lost control and won't be able to join in the fun so she eagerly suggests that Yodra sits with her back to Troy. This erotic position will allow Honey and Troy to satisfy Yodra, simultaneously.

Yodra submits to the request and climbs on top of Troy, straddling her legs over his. She slowly inserts all of Troy's hardness, sliding deep and deeper within. Yodra arches her back to better position herself to take all of him.

Thinking of blocking Honey from tasting Yodra, Troy takes one hand and plays with Yodra clit and the other hand caresses her breast. Troy speeds up his efforts to release by forcing Yodra to grind harder and harder and ride faster and faster.

Honey finds an opportunity to jump back in by taking both of Troy's hands and convincing him to caress Yodra's breast, exposing the rest of her sex for tasting.

As Troy thrusts in and out of Yodra, Honey licks the sides of him on the out strokes. Honey gently places Troy's jewels in her mouth, because she knows that's what he likes, and energetically rubs Yodra's clit.

Troy see's what Honey is trying to do so he decides it's time to put an end to this nightmare. He is ready to free Yodra from her increase of sexual tension by ruling her around her waist, adjusting him to go straight up and down. Going deep, hitting no walls, from the tip to the base with long, melodic strokes.

Honey tightly clamps around Troy's hardness, jacking him off on the up and down motions, as he attempts to get Yodra off. The loss of control causes Troy to release, she *catches* him in her mouth. Surprisingly, Yodra drops down on her knees to join in.

Honey's slickly connects eyes with Troy's while she and Yodra intimately taste Troy off of each other's face.

"Since your husband didn't quite finish the job, it will be my pleasure to top you off. I will be delighted in seeing you get yours, again," Honey adds, lightly pushing Yodra to lie on her back.

Honey sandwiches her face between Yodra's legs, feasting on her puffy lips. She repetitively slips two fingers within Yodra's slippery space, causing an exasperating exhale. Yodra and Honey moan and kiss and groan, as their twisted body's rock back and forth on the floor.

Yodra's noises grew intense, more rapid with faster pulses. Her face becomes a familiar expression of satisfying freedom. Yodra's back curves, her toes curl and her eyes roll back in her head as she frees herself.

Honey uses Nuki's method and squeezes Yodra clit between her fingers, unleashing a powerful stream to flow in her face.

Troy is so angry to witness this type of climax he storms out of the room and runs upstairs.

"Troy, wait a minute! What happened?" Yodra wails from the bottom of the staircase.

Slamming the bedroom door, Troy didn't say a word.

Yodra tearfully retreats back in the room where Honey was almost done putting on her clothes.

"I really don't know what's happening. I thought this was something my husband always wanted to do and I feel like I've done something wrong. I'm so sorry," Yodra embarrassingly admits.

"He'll be okay. Some men can't handle sexually losing control to a woman. Some can't accept that their women may actually be more satisfied from another woman. Unfortunately, this is the down side of the fantasy," she expertly explains.

The next sound we heard was a loud sound of a car horn, right in front of the house.

"I want that bitch out of my house, now!" Troy orders, storming past Yodra and Honey to the front door and holds it open.

"Troy, what happened? Did I do something wrong?" she begs again trying to get to the bottom of his sudden attitude and mood change.

"The control is back in my hands," Honey says, laughing hysterically as she walks past Troy to get out of the door.

CHAPTER 22
Under the Cover of Darkness

HONEY...

Still trying to process everything that happened the night before leaves me with the thoughts of what a night? All I see is the look on Troy's face playing over and over again in my head. I got him right where I want him and I am winning!

All of this drama has my soul restless this morning. I sat up slowly on the side of the bed. My stomach is cramping, my back is hurting, my head is throbbing and I'm feeling sick to my stomach. I have got to get my ass to the doctors and cut out some of this drinking.

I guess this can be morning sickness finally kicking in, when suddenly the urge to sit there was no more. I quickly jump up and run to the bathroom dropping to my knees and gripping the sides of this toilet, letting insides out. Evidently CeeCee heard me coughing and gagging because she came bursting in the bathroom.

"Honey, are you okay?" she asks, sitting right next to me on the floor and stroking my back for comfort.

"Yeah I'm okay, I guess the morning sickness has finally started," I reply while gagging.

"Do you need some water or something?" she questions, wetting a cold face cloth to put on the back of my neck.

"Yes," I barely respond, still letting the rest of what was on my empty stomach out.

"Uh oh, Honey, I'm afraid to tell you that it's not morning sickness," she informs after something stops her at the bathroom door.

"Why do you say that?" I ask with frustration in my voice.

"You appear to have had an accident last night is why," she replied pulling the sheets off of the bed.

"Oh, noooo!" I cry out. "Now what am I supposed to do? How am I supposed to survive?" I request with tears streaming down my face.

"Honey, you've been so consumed with getting revenge on Troy that you haven't even thought about taking care of yourself, have you? You smell like you had quite a few drinks last night and I've offered to not only go to the doctors with you, but I told you I would put you on my medical insurance plan to cover the expenses."

"I know plenty of girls who don't go to the doctor immediately and drink and smoke their entire pregnancy. I just thought I had time once I got Troy right where I want him."

"Maybe you weren't even pregnant, just late, have you thought about that? You've been under so much stress I can see why your hormones would be thrown off a little. How late were you anyway?"

"About a month or so and remember one of the pregnancy test did say positive," I respond pleading my case.

"Right and one said negative, remember? Bottom line, this whole situation about you getting pregnant by a married man, and trying to destroy his life to make yours better, just wasn't right in the first place," she criticizes. "I'm sorry, Baby, but you needed to hear it. Anyway, how did things go yesterday?" she investigations.

"Well, if you must know it didn't go as planned. In fact, it went in a whole other direction, but I don't even want to talk about that right now."

"It really didn't feel so good telling a woman that you are messing around with her husband did it?" she asks sounding cynical.

"Like I said I didn't even have to go there but I am, however, a little curious to know how would it make you feel if you had to do it, too?" I ask sarcastically.

"If I had to do what?" she asks looking puzzled.

"How would you feel if you were forced to tell her husband that you were messing around with his wife?" I say then just sat there searching her face for some type of reaction.

"Whaaat? What in the hell are you talking about, Honey?" she implies acting nervous and guilty.

"Yeah, you remember that new *love* interest that you just couldn't seem to tell me about just yet because its *sooo* complicated? I state putting my fingers up in the air mimicking air quotation marks. "You remember that don't you?"

"Yeah and…" she hesitantly answers.

"Well, you're one to judge, Ma'am. I put the pieces of your strange twisted love sexcapade together and I know about you and Yodra," I notify about my findings as she just sat there motionless. "CeeCee, did you hear me? What do you have to say about that?" I then ask in a dramatic whisper.

"But, how did you…"

"I figured out your dirty little secret. And all of this time you've called me selfish, don't you think your actions were just as selfish?"

"Damn, I don't even know what to say. You found me out. Hell, you found us out."

A Taste Of Honey   Ravry Sloan

"How come you didn't tell me when I first told you about me and Troy? You've had plenty of time to tell me the truth and you didn't. That shit is so grimy!" express Honey.

"I know I can be critical at times, especially with you, but I didn't want to be on that receiving end. There are no good reasons for my lies. I am embarrassed that I chose to be in a sticky situation with a married woman then judge you for the same thing.

"I thought I made better decisions than that and it happened before I even knew it. We both got caught up in our lonely, desperate emotions and our excited passion for photography.

"We both fell and we fell hard, catching one another, holding one another, comforting one another. She was open for what I had to offer and I was open to teaching her and here we are…there it is."

"I must admit I was very shocked to find out that your were not only messing around with a married woman but with my man's wife. Talking about a weird chain of events?"

"I guess like the old saying goes, it really is a small world, huh?" she questions looking ashamed.

"Yeah, I saw you were trying to call her yesterday so what were you going to do, warn her of my plans or something?"

"Honey, I was just trying to spare her that severe heart ache that I knew was about to come to her. I just don't understand the joy you have in destroying other people's lives on purpose. I mean none of us are perfect but you plan and plot to destroy families and change lives and that's scary."

"You know what? I'm 'bout sick of this shit! At least I am honest with myself about myself, but you on the other hand seem to be the one in denial. You walk around here like you're so perfect but you're f'cking around with someone married, too!

"You really ain't no better than me or anybody else for that matter! Maybe you need to take a good long look in the mirror at yourself before you start analyzing what other people do, especially when you're doing the same f'cked up shit!

"You really ain't shit either because you do all your shit under the cover of darkness but I'm going to be the one to bring

148

this shit to the light. You just watch me," I shout as I got up and get myself together.

"You know what? F'ck you, Honey! All of the shit I do for you and this is how you treat me?" hollers CeeCee.

"F'ck me? Well, f'ck you, CeeCee! Some friend you are, you've betrayed me and lied to me in my face all of this time and I think that's very hypocritical! I know I'm not perfect but I damn sho' don't go around judging people who don't think or act like me. I accept people for who and what they are, f'cked up or not!"

CHAPTER 23
Twist of Fate

YODRA...

I left the house pretty early to run errands, before heading to pick-up Ivory-Jade from the airport. I'm still confused about the night before, especially how it ended. Troy seems very upset and he refuses to explain his nasty attitude.

This is not at all how I imagine fulfilling his fantasy would be with Troy. Something went terribly wrong and I need get to the bottom of it. Troy reacted immediately! A cab arrived, in which seemed like minutes, and in the blink of an eye Sinclair was gone,. We did not exchange contact information so how am I going to talk to her?

As my husband, I was looking for Troy to come to me and be truthful about *whatever*. I feel like he's being dishonest about something.   Maybe he knows Sinclair? I just need to uncover this shit on my own.

.

I'm really not in the mood to deal with Corbyn right now. I see she called me all yesterday and has started again this morning. I know I asked her if she would help me with my show but this is ridiculous.   What in the world does Corbyn Carter want, I was thinking, answering my cell?

"Hello," I say trying not to sound too distracted.

"Hello, Yodra, how have you been, Love?" she asks, direct and straight to the point.

"I've been well, how have you been?"

"I can't complain. Are you busy?" she ask getting the formalities out of the way rushed and aggressively.

"I'm sorry I've been missing your calls, but what's been up? What's going on?"

"I thought you were purposely ignoring me or something. Do you think you can stop by sometime today or maybe we can meet somewhere? I really need to talk to you about something very, very important."

As eager as I was to find out what Corbyn wants to talk me about, I was on a mission to find this Sinclair and see what's really going on.

"Well, does it have to be today? Today is a very busy day for me. I on my way to pick up Ivory-Jade up from the airport and her party is today.

"Oh yeah, I mustn't forget about my big show Tuesday. So as you can see I have a very busy and hectic couple of days. Can this wait and maybe we can do this later on this week?"

"Do you even miss me?" she asks changing the whole tone and subject of the conversation.

"I do, I can't stop thinking about you," I disclose.

"Really? Well why is it I haven't heard from you? You haven't even picked up the phone to call me or even attempt to send me a text or anything," she replies, still hearing the aching in her voice.

"You're treating me like I did something to you to hurt you and I didn't. You're the one who made the decision to end things with me for your sorry ass husband," she unveils.

"Well, Corbyn, I'm sorry that you feel that way. I can't be the woman you expect me to be so the best thing for us, as bad as it hurts, is to just let things just be."

"What had you so preoccupied yesterday that you couldn't answer just one of my calls anyway?" she curiously inquires. "You know that I'm dying without you but it will destroy me if you were to ever be involved with another woman."

"Now that's really none of your business, Corbyn. Well, is Honey still staying with you?" I ask, re-directing the attention from me and my business to her and her business.

"Where in the hell did that come from? Why are you so curious about Honey all of a sudden?"

"Well, if you can ask about my business I can ask about yours," I respond boldly.

"As a matter of fact yes she is and since you're the one who brought her up she is the reason that I am calling you in the first place."

"Not now, Corbyn, I really have a lot to do and I can't handle any more drama on my plate let alone your drama, too! I promise I will call you as soon as things settle down and you can talk all about your little girlfriend."

"That's not it at all, Yodra. As I've stated several times before Honey is not my girlfriend anymore. We are like best friends. I can't understand why this is so hard for you to understand. I had my own personal life before you, why won't you understand that?"

"Okay, so you say, Corbyn, but as long as she is living with you and you are taking care of her in my eyes she is your girlfriend. Look, like I said, I am very busy and I don't have time or energy to deal with this today. I have to go but I promise I'll call you, I promise I will."

"Okay, please don't forget, this is very important. I do want you to know if, by chance, you change your mind or get a little free time between now and then; I'll be home all day.

"Am I still invited to your showing?" she asked before ending the conversation.

"Of course, you're still invited, but please don't bring that drama on my day, okay?"

"I wouldn't do you like that. I miss you so much Yodra Wilkins, more than you'll ever know. And I love you," she creepily expresses before hanging up.

Now, let me think…let me think back to the matter at hand, how can I track down this Sinclair? Okay, let me see…because the cab was at the house so quickly, Troy probably called his uncle. Uncle Rufus drives for Midnight Blue Taxi and that would at least explain the speedy arrival.

"Hello, is Rufus Jarvis there?" I ask after the dispatcher picks up.

"No, he's out on a fare, would you like his cell phone number or would you like to leave a message?"

"Well, wait a minute, maybe you can help me out," I state not wanting Troy to find out what I am doing in the first place.

"Go ahead ask away young, Lady."

"How can I find out if a customer was picked up by your company and the destination? Let me explain why I'm asking before you think I'm a stalker or something," I clarify with a lie, as we both laugh.

"I had a business presentation for a potential client here at my house last night, and I'm not exactly sure what company she called to pick her up. She left her cell phone and I want to return it to her but I have no earthly idea how to communicate with her.

"I feel as if I don't at least attempt to return her cell phone this could possibly jeopardize my whole business. Sir, can you help me with that? Please, Sir, please? It would really mean a lot to me," I implore.

154

After a short hesitation he replies, "Okay, I guess I can do that. Just tell me the address of pick-up and also around the time of the pick-up and a number I can call you back on. It will only take a few minutes.

"Okay, great!" After giving the dispatcher all of the information he requested I quietly sit in my car, stiffened with anticipation as all I can do is wait.

The time lag causes a sinking feeling in the bottom of my stomach. My woman's intuition kicks in warning me that in some kind of way Troy and Sinclair are connected.

After a few minutes my cell phone rings.

"Hello, Ma'am, you were absolutely correct, this pick-up was made by one our drivers. The place of drop off was at The Peacock Palisades, 1524 Royal Place, an apartment complex near midtown. He can't remember the apartment number but he thinks it is the second driveway after entering into the complex. I hope this helps and good luck on your business deal," he adds with a chuckle.

I didn't even say thank you, I just hung up the phone. My entire body went numb, frozen with amazement thinking that this cannot be just a mere twist of fate. I knew exactly where this place was and I was hoping that this wasn't the beginning of a real life nightmare.

CHAPTER 24
The Tables Turn

TROY...

I'm going to have to put an end to all of this foolishness. This Honey situation is really getting out of hand. I'm not going to believe out of all of the women in the world that Yodra just *happened* to meet Honey, impossible. And, I still need to handle this bullshit with Mello, too!!

"Daddy, Daddy," screams Ivory-Jade bursting through the front door. "Did you miss me?"

"There's my favorite little lady, how are you? And yes I did miss you!" I act surprised as we hug tightly.

"Daddy, I had so much fun! I'm so excited to be home and to be able to have my birthday pool/slumber party. Mama told me that the party will start at four and all of my friends will be here," she excitedly states.

"I know, the decorators are busy at work in the back getting everything ready for you and the chef and DJ are on their way.

"You've gotten so big, I almost didn't recognize you. It seems like you were gone forever!" I tease making her laugh hysterically. "Did you miss us?"

"So if you didn't recognize if it was me why did you give me a hug?" she asks with a silly look on her face.

"How could I forget that pretty little face," I say whining as I place my forehead on hers.

"You're so silly; Daddy and I sure did miss you! Grandma and Grandpa told me to tell you hello and to thank you for letting me come and spend the first half of my summer with them."

"Hey, Troy," speaks Yodra as she walks through the door. "It looks like everything is on track for the party this evening. The girls should start arriving around three but I have a few more errands to run. Can you two handle everything?" Yodra asks.

"I guess I really don't have a choice do I? You will be back in time for everything won't you?" I insist not really wanting to deal with this but wanting to deal with my own mess.

"Of course I will, why would you ask me that?" she questions with a cold, blank expression weighing heavy on her face.

"It seems to me that you would have had all of your errands taken care of before today is all I'm saying."

"What have you done to help me with this party anyway, Troy?" she states now giving me nothing but attitude.

"Hell, I paid for it," I reply turning my back on her and walking outside to the pool area with Ivory-Jade.

I was trying not be pissed off because this party shit is Yodra's idea. But just seeing the excitement on Ivory-Jade's face is enough to calm me down for now.

The chef finally arrives and begins firing up the grill and preparing food in the outside kitchen. The decorators were still blowing up balloons and setting up everything.

Ivory-Jade is talking a mile a minute. I try to act like I am listening but my mind keeps wandering right back to the night before.

The chef suddenly informs me that somebody was at the front door impatiently knocking and ringing the doorbell. It's kind of early the guests to arrive so I'm wondering who it can be.

"Troy!" screams Honey from the other side of the door. "I know you're in there, open up!" she yells even louder continuing to aggressively bang on the door.

"Bitch, you got some nerve coming back to my damn house! What in the f`ck do you want? You are not welcome here!"

"I need to talk to you, Troy. After seeing how you're living you cannot just throw me away like this! You don't love me anymore? I thought what we had was a good thing, right?" she says trying to look pitiful.

"Love you, are you serious? Bitch, I never loved you! I don't know what kind of games you're playing but you got me f`cked up! I don't know how you did it but I know tricked my wife into having a threesome with us, I know you did."

"I didn't have to fool anybody your wife came to me. She invited me because obviously you aren't satisfying her sexually. I decided to take advantage of the opportunity and my...my... my, was she good...and tasty, too!"

I lost control and found the back of my hand slapping her across her face causing her to stumble a little bit.

"That's all you got?" she gathers up to say, wiping the blood from her nose.

She then pulls a big manila envelope out of her bag. I was curious to what she had to show me I let her speak.

"First of all," she says coughing, trying to catch her breath, "I know about your son with Juicy."

"Bitch, that's old news. I don't have to tell you my business."

"Yeah, but how will your precious little wifey react if she found out you got a baby from a f`cking stripper?

159

A Taste Of Honey   Ravry Sloan

"And I can't prove it but I know you're the one who had something to do with her being strung out on drugs. Juicy maybe ghetto but she ain't that dumb or desperate enough to get f'cked up like this."

"Well, if you must know Yodra knows about my son, so this bit of information is only new news to you. And I don't have shit to do with her ass being on damn drugs. Now get the f'ck out of my house and don't ever come back here again before I make your ass disappear," I command, pointing my finger on her forehead and pushing her head back.

"Okay, but I bet she doesn't know about this," she said as she pulled out the photos that were in the envelope.

The pictures look like scenes from a sex orgy and then I recognize the room. They were pictures from Mello's Private Party. It was me having sex with Jamaica and that little guy, *Omar*.

"What the f'ck is this? What in the hell type bullshit are you playing, Honey? This is the kind of shit that could get your ass killed!" I scream, tearing the photos up in my hand.

"Oh, don't go to sweatin' now, Fool! I got yo' ass! Little Miss Wifey's little husband is not only f'cking me, the woman you guys' had a threesome with, but that you also like f'cking men and transvestites? Take a look at those photos again; Miss Jamaica is really Mr. Jamaica. Yeah, now look at how the tables have turned."

"What in the f'ck! I knew I was drugged!" I shout thinking; this is the bullshit Mello had up his sleeve.

Not really knowing how to react to these photos the only thing I say is, "I could kill your ass right now!"

"So now do you want to rethink throwing me away and loving me like you're supposed to?" she ask sarcastically.

"Bitch, have you lost your mind! So what, this shit is suppose to make me take you back?" Are you supposed to be blackmailing me? Never will I give in to this silly ass shit, you ain't worth it!

160

A Taste Of Honey   Ravry Sloan

"Yodra and I are recommitting to our marriage. We are focusing on our future, not the problems from our past. Everything I've done in the past is forgiven because that's the loving, faithful wife I have. We will work together, as husband and wife."

"Ha, I really thought you were a smart man but you are really, really dumb. She is really making you look like a damn fool," she express joyfully.

"You know what? It's time for you to leave, Little Girl," I calmly state trying to close the door in her face.

"Wait!" she yells, standing so the door wouldn't close. "Tell Yodra to come out here, too! I have got to see the expression on both of your faces when I say this," she laughs ecstatically.

"She's not here. So, leave! Bye!"

"Well let's just see about what this *little girl* has to tell you about your, faithful wife.

"Bitch, you better get the f'ck out of my house," I scream putting my hands around her neck and using all my strength and pressure to choke the shit out of her.

"Daddy, Daddy, what are you doing?" shouts Ivory-Jade standing behind me looking horrified at what she was witnessing.

I quickly let Honey's neck go forcing her to fall to her knees to catch her breath. I stand there mortified that my daughter is observing what I am doing.

"Nothing, Baby, go on back outside to the pool area, she's just a friend. We were just playing, now go on now; I'll be there in a minute."

Honey was still on her knees, coughing and looking up at me with an evil look in her eyes.

"Troy, you will pay for this! You haven't seen or heard the last from me. You just mark my words you f'cking dog!"

I can't handle her way I really want to so I cough up spit then spit it on her, slamming the door.

I can't get those photos out of my mind. Bits and pieces of that night really start coming back to me. I now remember seeing flashes in that room. I had to be drugged in order for this shit to be played off so well. What in the hell have I gotten myself into?

161

How am I going to explain all of this shit to Yodra? This is some real bullshit!

"Daddy, who was that lady at the door," asks Ivory-Jade, looking shaken up and scared to death.

"It will be okay, Sweetheart, she was just a friend looking for your mom and she was choking. I was trying to help her breath, Baby, its okay I promise. Are you okay?" I ask trying to comfort her and think how I can make her not tell Yodra.

"Yes, but it looked like you were choking her," she replies with the anxiety releasing from her face.

"Nooo, Baby, I wasn't choking her I was helping her because *she* was choking."

"But I thought I heard yelling?" she questions some more.

"You did, but it was not that kind of yelling. I was panicking because I couldn't get her to breathe fast enough and she was turning blue in the face. She's okay now and it's all over with. So are you excited about your party?" I askes trying to change the subject and re-direct her focus back the party.

"I sure am. I'm ready for my friends to come and mama to come back."

"I'm sure you are. Look, Ivory-Jade, I don't see any reason why we have to tell your mama about this little incident right now. I'll tell her later. If you tell her right now she's going to worry about her friend and she may end up cancelling your party to go see about her. I know you don't want that, do you?"

"No, but why would she cancel my party because her friend started choking?" she asks innocently enough.

"Because she will be sad and she won't be in a good mood for your party. Since you really didn't see what happened let me just tell her okay?"

"Okay. Is your friend going to the hospital?"

"She probably will so the doctors will check on her so don't you worry your little self about it okay? Now, let's go back out by the pool and see if the decorators are done, I'll race you," I say fooling her and trying to gain total control of this situation.

A Taste Of Honey   Ravry Sloan

   I can't believe that bitch came to my house to blackmail
me. I'm so pissed right now. I refuse to let the sun go down
without me putting my hands on that muthaf'cking Mello.

A Taste Of Honey   Ravry Sloan

CHAPTER 25
Confirm or Deny?

HONEY...

    I sat in the back of the taxi, motionless and in shock. Every now and then I can still taste the bitter taste of the blood from my nose draining to the back of my throat. I need to refocus and create a better plan than this.

    Why am I being so vindictive? Why can't I leave this man alone? What is wrong with me?

    "Ma'am, Miss, where would you like me to take you now?" asks the taxi driver still waiting on me to give him my next stop.

    "Did you see what that bastard did to me?" I inquire.

    "No, Ma'am, I didn't see anything. Where do you want to go," he asks again unsympathetic.

"Do you know where Splitz is?" I request feeling embarrassed.

Nuki is the only person I can think of who will be here for me right now. I can't trust CeeCee anymore.

As luck would have it Big Nuki was walking towards the front door of the club as we pulled up.

"Hey, stop right here," I instruct the driver, pulling up next to Nuki.

"Hey, what's going on? Oh, it's you, Stranger," Nuki states identifying me as I let my window down to speak.

"Hey, I really need your help. I don't have anywhere else to turn. Can you please help me?" I beg Nuki as if my life depends on it.

After feeling her eyes piercing my battered face she finally replies and pays the driver.

"Yeah, come on with me," she responds, taking me to her private office.

"Thank you so much, Nuki, I really appreciate this," I humbly thank her help me cleaning myself up.

"So, are you ready to tell me what's going on now? What happened to your face and who did this to you?" she asks sitting on the edge of her desk, already knowing the answer.

"Oh, Nuki, all this shit has blown up in my face," I say mimicking a whiny baby, leaning into her chest to have direct body contact.

"Do you want me to take you to the emergency room?" she quizzes, with her arms still wrapped tightly around me.

"Yes, I think my nose may definitely be broken," I explain trying to hold back tears.

"I told you I had you and I would treat you better than them niggas out there in the streets, remember?" she whispers in my ear reminding me of her past proposal.

"You were right," is all I could say, walking to her BMW truck.

It is a silent ride on our way to urgent care.

A Taste Of Honey   Ravry Sloan

"So are you ready to tell me what happened?" asks Nuki again, as we sit in the waiting area after getting checked in.

"All I know how to do is shake my ass, f'ck and suck. So I quickly make it to the top by nothing but my good looks and skills. I thought I was doing something and I made something of myself.

"Think about it. This handsome millionaire could not get enough of me, and he had the choice of hundreds of women, but he chose me! I guess I created a fantasy world I hoped would come true.

"I was too embarrassed to see the truth and I just desperately wanted to make him see that he really does love me. I believed we could be one big happy family, especially thinking that a baby maybe on the way.

"The reality is he is not trying to leave his wife. He took everything back he gave me, which was my new way of life and I just can't allow that.

"When you come from *nothing* and you get a taste of *something*, you don't want to go back to that old life style. The blackmail with the pictures didn't seem to work and when I got the courage to go and tell his wife she invited me to join them in a threesome, can you believe that?" I state venting out the dilemma.

"Whaaat? That's what's up?" she replies snickering a little.

"Yeah, she asked me if I wanted to play some sex games with her and Troy, so I figured why not. Just in case she's suspected who I was I gave her a fake name. I reached out to Troy a few times but he refused to hear me out. So when I saw another opportunity to get back at him I took it.

"I made that wifey of his shake a few times and I did manage to make him shake, too," I brag as we both laugh.

We chit-chatted a bit more, loosening up about each other, until they call my name to go to the back. Surprisingly, she came back with me so I will not have to do this alone.

I answer honestly about the possibility of being pregnant. But the hospital has a policy in place to protect them from lawsuits so I still had to take a pregnancy test.

Nuki and I sit, waiting on the test results cracking jokes, laughing, and flirting a little.

"What if you are pregnant, what's the plan?" she asks turning our playful conversation into something more serious.

"I don't know, Nuki. After this morning I don't think there's a chance in hell of me being pregnant. I know Troy, he ain't never gone do right.

"I'll help you. I've told you before that I was really feeling you and I'm looking for a strong woman like you by my side to help me with this empire. Don't be afraid, step out of the box and let me take care of you, even if you are pregnant," she expresses confidently holding my hands.

"What? Are you for real? I don't even know you. How do I know you're for real?" I ask very doubtful.

"I'm here aren't I? Have I ever not come through for you since you met me? Have I not made you feel good? And clearly you must trust me, even if it's a little bit. You came to me when you had nowhere else to go. Come on, Lil'Baby, give me a chance and let me take care of you?" she passionately asks.

Before I can answer the nurse comes back with the results and congratulates me on becoming a mama. I sat there in disbelief because after this morning how?

"Are you sure I'm pregnant?" I ask boldly and loudly.

"Yes, Ma'am, you're pregnant. You are bleeding so you are definitely going to need to schedule an appointment with your obstetrician as soon as possible. Or I can provide you with the information for planned-parenthood, but for now we can still give you the x-ray for your nose."

I'm pregnant! Pregnant? This is unbelievable! I still have a chance to get what I want from Troy's ass after all. But I can't do Nuki like this. She is so nice and seems to genuinely want to take care of me.

"So? What do you say? Can I have the chance to make you and this baby happy? This would mean so much to me. This is just how I want things to go for me. You don't need shit from that dude, I got everything. Let's just move forward and let me show you what I can do," she states arguing her point.

"I really don't know what to say," I reply.

"Say yes!" she encourages.

"Okay, yes, Nuki, yes! Let's see what damage we can do to the world," I answer as we both laugh and kiss.

"So, where have you been staying?" she asks as we leave the doctors.

"I've been staying with my ex-lover since Troy put me out of the loft. We are just friends nothing more and my personal things are at her condo and my other, bigger things are in a storage closet."

"Okay, so we need to stop by there and get your stuff now then. I have some business I need to take care of at the club so after we get your stuff I'll drop you off at my place to get fancied up then we'll stop by and holla' at Mello."

"Sounds good to me," I reply. "Besides I need to tell him about Troy's reaction to the photos. He was mad as hell, talkin' bout he knew he was drugged. The look on his face was priceless," I express playfully.

"I hope that clown won't go over there trying to do something to my brother. He needs to learn to practice self-control when he leaves home. That nigga just mad he got caught with his pants down, literally," she jokes, falling out laughing again.

"Maaan, he got caught up. He was looking so hard because he couldn't believe he was in those photos. He was caught having a threesome with pretty much with two other men.

"And not to mention me being a part of a threesome with played in. Troy has crossed so many lines that when his wife learns of everything he's going to be so f'cked. His perfect little life will be destroyed, crumbled right before his eyes. Now he will see exactly how I feel. The shame, the rejection and the abandonment

CHAPTER 26

Confronting your Fears

YODRA...

I know this party is important to Ivory-Jade but I cannot relax until I find out for myself who this Sinclair really is.

I know the exact location where Sinclair was dropped off by the driver. It seems like a mighty big stretch to assume it is a coincidence this is the where Corbyn lives, too! I understand that Corbyn is hurt but why go to such extremes to hurt me?

Well, she said she'd be home all day, I say out loud eyeing her bike in its regular parking space. I walk towards her condo and call her on the intercom.

"It's me..."

"Come on up, the door is open," Corbyn answers.

My heart pounds like a bass drum and my knees vigorously shake as I climb the stairs.

"Hey, You," she speaks, hugging me tightly as she opens the door. "I've missed you so much. I didn't expect to see you, especially since you said you would be too busy. Either way I'm glad you made time for me," she explains taking my hand and guiding me to sit on the chocolate leather sofa in the living room.

"Is that right? What's going on, Corbyn?" I flat out ask suspiciously.

"What do you mean? I'm a wreck is what's going on! It's been really hard not talking to you every day and not seeing your beautiful face. There is so much I've wanted to tell you. I've been keeping secrets from you and it's killing me not to let you know what's been going on," Corbyn reveals.

"Oh, really now, just what kind of secrets have you been keeping?" I inquire.

"Well, Yodra, there is something important I really need to talk to you about," she informs as I prepare to finally hear the truth.

"Okay, you've read my mind, that is exactly why I'm here, to hear what you have to tell me," I answer trying not to sound too anxious.

"What I have to talk to you about is about Troy," she defines as the whole tone of the conversation changes.

"Troy? What about Troy?" I ask inquisitively.

"It's been an inner struggle for me to tell you or to not get in the middle of this situation. Unfortunately, obstacles have presented themselves which brought me to a decision to go ahead and tell you."

"Spit it out already! What is it? Just tell me?" I impatiently squeal.

"Well, you know I told you before that Honey and I broke up because of her wanting to be with this guy she met instead of me, right?"

"Right and..." I reply as my heart seems like it was exploding inside of my chest.

I already began putting the pieces together of what I thought she was going to say.

172

"Well, I found out that Troy was that man. They met at the strip club where Troy frequented and Honey worked..." she begins explaining.

"Are you serious?" I question with tears building up in my eyes.

"Yes, I am. The whole reason Honey ended up here with me in the first place was because Troy beat her up and put her out of the loft he had for her.

"I know it is selfish but I didn't want to ruin what we had so I decided not to tell you. What good did that do because I still lost you."

I am having a hard time processing all of this new information coming at me so quickly. Sitting in a comatose state of mind I forget all about asking Corbyn if my gut was right about Sinclair and Honey being the same people. After hearing about Troy and Honey's infidelity makes me feel too ashamed to even mention that we all may have engaged in a threesome.

I look like a real idiot. I must face it, I got played and I don't even know if it is Troy, Corbyn, or Sinclair; or whoever she really may be.

At least this helps clear up Troy's bad attitude about this whole confusing situation. I was in shock, but not because he cheated, because he was abusive to her and was taking care of her. Out of all of the years that I've know Troy these actions are totally out of his character. My body went numb as a thousand thoughts ran through my mind.

"How long have you known about Troy and Honey messing around?" I ask mentally trying to avoid who really and truly wronged me.

"I first found out about them when Honey came to me needing somewhere to live," she explains.

"So, why where you calling so adamantly for yesterday? What was so special about yesterday if you've know about them before now?" I ask frantically wanting answers"

"Before I answer that I need to say this. I've only loved two women in my life, that's you and Honey, and I lost both of you to the same damn guy!

"I am angry that Troy disrespects you and doesn't make you happy. And I am angry for him hurting Honey the way she's hurting. You just don't know the thoughts I had to hurt the both of you.

"I still can't believe you chose him over me. I feel like you never really loved me and you found one little thing to end it with us. You didn't even fight for us," she tearfully uncovers.

"I'm so sorry I made you feel that way but we both knew we made selfish decisions for our own selfish satisfaction. I may have complained about my unhappiness in my marriage but not one time did I give you any indication that I may leave my husband for you.

"I may have taken for granted you agreed to your role in what we were doing and I see now that you didn't. You knew I was married when we first met, meaning you supplied what Troy lacked. I didn't see it ending, but I also didn't see it being happily ever forever either," I state.

"That's sad because I saw a future with us. Every dream I had you were right by my side," she shares.

"Corbyn, you are the best thing that ever happened to me but I am not willing to give up my family. Is this why you were calling me like that?" I asks not understanding the urgency in telling me that.

"No, I was calling to tell you that Honey was on her way to confront you at the spa and I wanted to warn you. I thought that maybe if you were prepared for what she was about to do so the blow wouldn't be so hard," she explains.

"This is too scary and complicated. I am so confused that I really don't know what to do, feel or think right now. Corbyn, I have to go! I need to get back before the guest arrive and the party gets started."

"When will I talk to you again?" she ask, heading towards the door.

"Right now, Corbyn, I don't know," I reply trying to get my mind back focused on the events that will carry over the next few days.

"Can I still see you Tuesday?" she request walking up behind and rubbing my shoulders.

"I'll let you know," I inform.

"I still want to help you prepare for your debut exhibit. I know how important this is for you and I also know old undependable Troy won't be there helping you either. I want nothing but the best for you and you know I will do everything in my power to make the best always happen for you.

"How's the big day coming along anyway?" she then asks, already sensing a disconnect to the whole conversation.

"It's going surprisingly well, thanks for asking. The framers will deliver the photographs to the aquarium tomorrow morning and their organizers will help me set-up the displays by noon. It seems like everything is going as scheduled."

"Are you excited?" she probes with excitement in her voice ignoring.

"Despite everything going on, very much so, it's been a long time coming. Honestly I could not have done it without you. I would personally like to thank you for mentoring me. Also, for encouraging me to have a keen eye for beauty, allowing me to convey a story with my work. I've learned to speak to the soul from my eyes to your eyes," I express, beginning to cry uncontrollably.

"No need to thank me for that passion you already possessed. I just helped you believe in yourself just as I believe in you. I forced you to confront your fears and embrace your confidence. I knew you could do it and I'm so proud of you for finally allowing others to see your story," she inspires, holding me tightly in her arms.

"Thank you," I modestly reply in her ear, recognizing her capability to still hypnotize me by just her tender cuddles and affection.

175

"It's all going to be okay, trust me. I will make it all better for my Baby, I always do. I got your back more than you know. Don't worry about that Troy and Honey business. I'll make sure they don't hurt you anymore."

"On second thought, maybe coming to my show may not be the best thing to do right now. I appreciate your wanting to help but I think I really need to do this by myself," I express as I clean my teary face.

"I understand if you don't want me to come but I want you to know that I'm not happy about it, I'm not happy at all. Please reconsider, Baby. I really want to be there to support you and your dreams, please say you'll think about it and not just say no, okay?" she pleads.

"Okay, Corbyn, I will think about it. I have to go."

CHAPTER 27
Busted!

TROY...

The guests are arriving and Yodra hasn't made it back yet! I wonder what's taking her so damn long. It's not like her to wait until the last minute to run errands, particularly something for Ivory-Jade.

I'm eager to leave myself and go find that Mello. What kind of nigga does some underhanded grimy shit like this? Just for a bitch to try and blackmail me, I don't understand the reasoning behind this..

I hope that Ivory-Jade can keep her mouth shut about that whole Honey fiasco. I hate my baby saw me lose my temper and self-control like that, especially with another woman at my home.

A Taste Of Honey   Ravry Sloan

"Mr. Wilkins, would you like for us to go ahead and get started?" asks one of the moms, with the backyard already full of excited and anxious little girls, boys and moms.

"Sure, go ahead. Yodra should be back shortly. I can't imagine why she's not here," I express trying to hold in my frustrations about the incident with Honey, Ivory-Jade seeing me lose control and that Yodra is just not here so I can leave. Just as I was about to call her on her cell phone she pops in the door as if it were a regular day.

"Hey, is everybody here?" she asks nonchalantly.

"What do you think? Where in the hell have you been?" I now ask sounding pissed and paranoid.

"Don't talk to me right now?" she demands as she rudely walks pass me towards the backyard.

"What the f'ck is wrong with you?" I ask grabbing her arm, curious to where she had been.

"Get your muthaf'cking hands off of me, Troy! I don't have time for this bullshit right now!" she screams as she snatches her arm from my grip.

"Well fine, f'ck it then, Yodra! Since this was your f'cking idea you do this damn party by your damn self! F'ck it, I'm out of this bitch!" I shout before I know it, storming out of the front door.

I really didn't mean to handle this situation like this with Yodra. She hasn't even done anything. I'm just not ready to deal with her attitude on top of everything else that is going on right now. I'll just have to deal with her later. I feel like my life is falling apart and I need to get to the bottom of what's happening!

After pulling up at Mello's Private Club I pull around back knowing where the other entrance to his office was. I only saw two cars and one was Mello's. I took a chance and let myself in through the wedged door. I follow the dark hall to a room on the end, with a light shining from under the half cracked open door.

"This guy is somewhat of a mystery. He's very manipulative and controlling and you're not even aware that you're in that position.

178

"For instance, I can't prove it but I know he had something to do with this stripper chick getting her hands on some bad drugs or something and which made her lose her mind," explains the familiar voice of Honey on the other side of the door.

"Do you mean Juicy from Pink Pussycats?" asks the male voice, which I confidently identify immediately as Mello's voice.

"Yes, do you know her?" Honey questions Mello sounding surprised.

"Yeah, you can say that. We've worked together before. Wow, that's f'cked up that he did that to that girl. That nigga Troy is hell and he'll pay for that shit eventually!"

"What does that mean?"

"Nothing…but yeah, go ahead now and tell your little story," he answers.

"Let me have his trifling ass first then you can have him and do whatever you like. I've put in too much work not to get what I want." she states laughing.

"Y'all should have seen his punk ass the other night. I got this nigga right where I want him, trust me. I can't wait until he finds out that his pretty little wifey has been switching teams when she goes out to play."

"What?" asks an unfamiliar female voice now speaking? "What in thee hell!" she loudly laughs in disbelief.

"What the f'ck?" ask Mello, chiming back in the conversation?

"Yes! Let me tell you the story how I know this is meant to be," states Honey as if she were boasting about her accomplishments.

"I was going to confront ole' wifey about this nigga Troy when she asked me out on a free spa date. I wanted to go to a spa anyway so I was not about to turn down a free offer and invitation, so I went. Before I could tell her about her husband and as fate would have it, she asked me home to participate in a threesome!"

"Get the f'ck out of here," states Mello laughing loudly.

"Yup! I was invited to have a threesome with my lover and his wife, by his wife. Mr. Troy Wilkins himself, her husband was

179

definitely in for a rude awakening. I couldn't have planned it better myself if I tried," she begins explaining this unforeseen ending of this story with amusement.

"Well, damn! I'm so jealous right now," Mellow expresses sounding very relaxed and envious.

"So, yeah I went home with her and we surprised the hell out of Troy. Of course, wifey was the idiot in the mix because she had no clue to who in the hell I really was, she was just damn clueless.

"But anyway, after we surprised Troy with this perfect plan I started noticing some strange connections in their house. Like one of my ex-lover's most famous and precious photographed pieces was hanging on their wall. CeeCee would never sell such a personal piece and not who the buyers are, but she never mentioned knowing either one of them.

"Initially I thought that was a fluke, but then ole' girl left her cell phone on the bar. I was left in the room alone and looked to see who was blowing her phone up like that and it was CeeCee. I mean four, five, six calls back to back. Not to mention all of the missed calls throughout the day.

"Then, Miss Thang brought her fine ass down stairs smelling all good. She mentioned it was a rare fragrance. CeeCee had on that fragrance before and when I asked her about it she told me the same thing. And that her sweetie sacrificed to give to her," Honey describes.

"Awe, man! What did she say when you asked her about it?" quizzes the other female voice.

"I didn't let her know I knew anything! I had both of them bitches right where I wanted them. Troy was so scared and pissed that I was in his house and f'cking his wife that he wouldn't dare let wifey know anything," Honey boasts, slapping hands together and laughter.

"Now this is some real soap opera shit. When I grow up…dammit man! You had the wife and the husband?" asks the confused sounding female voice.

"You're my hero!   No, you're my *shero*," loudly state Mello over all of the laughing.

"That nigga was trying to act like he didn't want to f'ck me and she was acting like she didn't know how to f'ck me…at first.

"Troy wanted to explode at the sight of me pleasing his wife but that wife was taking all of this. Troy couldn't handle it anymore and joined in, selectively, of course. He tried his best to keep me out of it but I made that bitch cum."

"Now this is some real shit! Did you get what you wanted out of it?" asks Mello?

"That night I did," she responds in enjoyment. "But the kicker is I still didn't get a chance to tell wifey about me and Troy so I'm going to just show up at her art exhibition at the Aquarium and surprise her on her big night. I think it's only fair that she knows the truth about her husband and the fact that I am having his baby," she announces.

"You're pregnant, too! Wow! Troy has really f'cked up this time. Well if destroying his life was your goal this should definitely do it!" exclaims Mello.

Then all of a sudden anger and resentment fills me and I was seeing red. My heart was hammering in my chest, I was beginning to feel light-headed and I start shaking a little from an overwhelming feeling of emotions.

"What in the fuck is going on here?" I scream, not being able to take hearing another word from Honey and kicks open the office door.

"Troy, what in the hell are you doing here?" asks Honey with the look of fear and surprise on her face.

"Speak of the muthaf'cking devil, here he is in the flesh, Mr. Troy Wilkins," states the guy looking girl with the braids, the other female voice I was hearing.

"Yeah, this is this muthaf'cka," answers Mello sarcastically. "Looks like he's a wee bit angry," he then says antagonizing me.

"What in the f'ck is going on here? What is all of this shit about?" I ask.

181

"Payback, Muthaf'cka, the big payback. I told you, you don't want to f'ck with me. I begged and pleaded with you to accept the terms of our break up, but oh no, you refused so I had to show your ass. I told you before I can show you better than I can tell you."

"So what, I'm supposed to be blackmailed into loving you again and being forced to take care of you? Really, Honey? Do you honestly think that this is the solution to all of your problems?

"And Mello, this is the punk shit you do? How could you be such a bitch and do such bitch, shit?" I demand wanting answers but couldn't stop shaking my head in disbelief at how all of this has just unfolded.

"You come in here like you're victim and somebody is supposed to feel sorry for you or something? You got life twisted, Troy, life just doesn't work the way that you want it to work.

"You must pay for the way that you treated me. I gave you the option of doing it willingly or forcibly, but either way you were going to have to commit. You took too long so I was forced to make the decision that worked best for me.

"You had the option, remember? Now sing that shit to somebody else who gives a f'ck and deal with it!" she so disrespectfully states while pushing my face with her whole, open hand.

Before I knew it we were tumbling across the room after I got my hands around Honey's neck, when the last thing I remember was us falling…

CHAPTER 28
Secret Obsession

HONEY...

"Oh my goodness, Mello, what did you do?" I shockingly ask as he and Nuki roll Troy from on top of me.

"I didn't touch that man. His clumsy ass did that on his own," he states taking Troy's pulse on the side of his neck. "He ain't dead, he'll be alright.

"I was trying to make sure you were alright! This is way too much and I really didn't expect this shit to get this far out of hand. Y'all need to get the hell out of here! Y'all need to go sit down somewhere for a little while and wait to hear from me. I'll take care of this mess!

"My sister don't need no more drama in her life or to get into any more trouble and be sent off to jail again, so go, bye!" he shouts as we run out the door. "I'll call you, Nuk, when the coast is clear," he instructs as the door shuts behind us.

"This wasn't supposed to happen! Too much is going wrong!" I state in a panic as I felt dizzy from the episode.

"You heard Mello, at least he ain't dead. Everything will be alright, trust me, Mello will take care of everything. He always does," Nuki assures trying to comfort my fears.

"But what if he dies? What if he just told us that to get us out of there? Nuki, I'm scared. I didn't think things would actually go this far, what am I suppose to do?" I ask in between my sobs.

"Everything will be alright, I promise," she calmly tries comforting me by stroking my hair. "Ok, here's the plan. We will grab a bite to eat and get a room downtown and chill out until we hear back from Mello."

"But we need to be doing something!" I scream.

"No, what you need to be doing is calm the f*ck down and chill! We'll be just fine."

It was nearly close to check-out time when Mello finally calls Nuki the next morning instructing us that we were safe and Troy was fine.

"So what's the plan now since we can finally make some moves?" asks Nuki after checking out of the hotel and we are in the car.

"Even though I'm furious with CeeCee right now it's only fair that I let her know what is going on. If you don't mind, could you please take me to her place?

"I really don't know how much Troy overheard but if he did hear me telling y'all about his wife and CeeCee he may be after her next, who knows? No telling what he may do. I hope he is alright though, Nuki. I didn't want the man to die!"

"Why do you even care what happens to CeeCee anyway? Wasn't your goal to ruin this man's life and not really give a f*ck who else got hurt in all of the mayhem?"

"Yes, but CeeCee is my friend. I don't really want to see her hurt in all of this, especially since she is in love with Troy's wife. I did more than enough to hurt her when we broke up I at least owe her that."

"If you say so, Honey, but I think CeeCee is a big enough girl to handle her own business. She decided to fool around with a married woman so heart-ache was bound to be in their future at some point is all I'm saying." Nuki puts out there.

"Yeah, but CeeCee has always been that person there for me when I had no one else to count on," I plead my case. "She doesn't deserve to be caught all up in me and Troy's business and I will try to spare her feelings as much as I can."

As we turn into CeeCee's drive-way I can see her pulling out on her motorcycle. "Dammit, that's her leaving now," I state.

"You want to try and catch her?" asks Nuki.

"Really? Did you see she was on a bike? Maaan, CeeCee rides that thang like she's being chased by the police or something."

"Do you still need to stop then?"

"Yes, I still have my key. I need to run up and grab a few more things. I'll be right back."

Entering the apartment I can see that CeeCee's computer still up and I can see she printed out the photos from my e-mail. How did this happen? She must have hacked into my e-mail account!

Then an odor of something burning from down the hall distracts me. What is that smell, I ask myself?

I curiously follow the aroma of the burning smell to CeeCee's room, through her closet to a surprised sitting room where I was shocked to see CeeCee's other alarming obsession.

There were hundreds of pictures of Yodra pinned all over the walls, ceilings and doors. A dark curtain hangs on the only window in the small dark sitting room. A shrine like alter, which looks like, keepsakes between her and Yodra were kept.

I notice pictures of Yodra and Troy but Troy's face was cut out. But after a few more seconds of looking at the collection of pictures I then notice pictures that were of Yodra with other people with their faces cut out, too!

What traumatize me are the pictures of me and Yodra from the fund raiser event and the spa with *my* face cut out! I think CeeCee has really lost her mind, I think quickly leaving the secret room.

But before leaving I notice knife blades puncturing through on the other side of the door. I close the door to look behind it and the first thing I see were all of the cut out heads from the pictures with Yodra nailed to the wall behind the door. The nails are going straight between the eyes of me and all of the different people.

The most disturbing image is several enlarged pictures of Troy's head pinned to the back of the door with the knives in them that looked as if there were thrown from across the room. The blades are going straight through the middle of his face on each picture. I ran out of the secret room so fast to the car with Nuki.

"What is it? What's wrong?" asks Nuki when I finally got in the car.

"You're not going to believe this but CeeCee at some point hacked into my e-mail address and saw copies of the pictures of Troy."

"What? What is she going to do with that?"

"I didn't know but trust me that its nothing compared to what I have to tell you about what I just saw. Very troubling," I reveal with fear and hesitation.

"What?" she demands.

"I just saw CeeCee's secret shrine of Yodra in her room."

"So, and…"

"No, you don't get it, Nuki, it was a real shrine! A dark, small room packed with dozens of candles and hundreds of pictures of Yodra taped everywhere, Nuki. The pictures were on the walls, the ceilings and the doors. The heads of me, Troy and a couple of other people I don't know were cut out of the pictures and nailed to another wall.

"But check this, she had several headshots of Troy with knives thrown through the center of his face," I finally expose the big shocker for last.

"Are you serious?" she asks in disbelief.

A Taste Of Honey   Ravry Sloan

"Yes! I guess this is a side of CeeCee I never knew about. Let me think…okay, I know what I need to do now. I need to find CeeCee and offer her a caring hand. I will say she may even be dangerous.

"First, let's start by going over to Troy's house! I feel like she may be headed there and I need to try and stop something bad from happening.

"Wait a minute, let me get this straight! You did all of this to get revenge on Troy for breaking up with you and now you want to save everybody that is involved? I don't understand you, Honey; you're a real piece of work."

"So what does that mean?"

"I just don't understand you having a conscience for the people who are on a path of your destruction…after that fact, but okay! If you want to go over to Troy's house then Troy's house is where we will go," she comments with an exuberant sigh, shaking her head.

After arriving at Troy's house and walking up to the door I can see the pictures thrown all over the yard, definite signs CeeCee was here. I knock on the door and simultaneously ring the doorbell. I yell but no one came to the door.

"So I take it she wasn't there?" asks Nuki after getting back in her truck.

"No, but look what was everywhere, the infamous pictures of Troy at the private party."

"Whaaat? Nooooo, wow! This thing is crazy. So what do you want to do now?" Nuki asks.

"I don't know. Ooh, yeah I forgot I have Yodra's number! I am going to call her."

"Good luck! This woman is not going to want to sit down and talk with you about her husband and her lover I can promise you that."

"When I tell her about CeeCee and her secret obsession with her she will be thankful I came to her," I confidently express.

187

CHAPTER 29

The Cat's Out of the Bag!

YODRA...

I can't believe Troy leaves Ivory-Jade's party and does not return. And to think, I was willing to give this marriage another chance but this is turning out to be a damn joke!

I have got to stop all of this crying and get it together. I have to get out of here.

"Ivory-Jade, I have an idea! Why don't we relocate the slumber part of the party to The Camelot Suites across the street from the aquarium?"

"You mean go to a hotel to spend the night?" she asks with clarification.

"Yes! How does that sound?"

"It sounds like it's going to be a lot of fun, Mama!" she replies with enthusiasm.

189

A Taste Of Honey   Ravry Sloan

I feel bad leaving the house the way we did but after checking my phone upon waking up Troy never attempted to call or text. Maybe I should have called, or at least texted, to let him know where we are so he wouldn't worry.

I do see where I missed several calls and text from Corbyn and an unknown number. I can't deal with her right now. I need to try and focus on my show tomorrow.

"I had fun last night, Mama, thank you!!" appreciates Ivory-Jade after all of her friends were picked up.

"You're welcome, Ivory-Jade."

"Did daddy ever come?"

"No, he never came. I'm sorry, Sweetheart."

"Do you think he knows where we are? He was probably worried, huh?" asks Ivory-Jade.

"No, he didn't call but we're not going to worry ourselves with that are we? Besides, since he hasn't called I think he is be okay," I acknowledge trying to re-direct her thoughts and control my shaky emotions.

"But I wonder why he didn't want to celebrate my birthday with me?"

"I'm sure he didn't mean to *not* come back to your party, Sweetheart. Your daddy probably got so busy that he couldn't make it back in time. You know daddy's work keeps him very busy sometimes. All that truly matters to me is that you had fun."

"Oh, yes, Mama, yes, I did!! I was so happy that all of my friends came and brought me gifts and we got to swim and play games and had a slumber party at the hotel! Thank you, Mama, for the best birthday ever!!"

"I'm glad you had fun, Sweetheart, I really am. I thought it was a great idea that we came downtown to stay at the hotel instead of the slumber party being at home, didn't you think?"

"Yes, but I hate Daddy didn't come. Is he mad at me or something?" she asks not understanding what is going on.

"I wish daddy would have come, too, and no, I don't think daddy is mad at you. It's not about you at all so why don't we worry about daddy later, but for right now mama's got a lot to do to get ready for my big unveiling tomorrow.

"Besides I think us staying at the hotel just makes things so much easier for me and my unveiling," I try explaining the sudden move.

"Is there a pool?" she asks still looking to have a good time.

"Yes, it sure does, but guess what?" I request, encouraging more excitement.

"What? My daddy is coming?" she states excitedly.

"No, but I have something just as good. Emerson's mother is going to come back so you and Emerson can go to the pool and spa and really have a good time while I take care of this last minute setting up stuff. How do you like that?"

"That sounds like it's going to be fun! I only wish daddy was here."

"I know, Sweetheart. I will make sure I let him know where you are and that he needs to get down here and spend some time with you or at least call, okay?

"The framers will be here in a couple of hours so I have to get dressed. I promise I won't leave until Emerson and her mom get here, okay?" I say assuring her that her fun will continue.

"Okay, I like hanging out with Emerson because she is my best friend. You know what? I think I know where daddy went!" she recollects with excitement.

"Where, Ivory-Jade?" I ask curiously.

"Maybe daddy went to the hospital to check on your friend," she states innocently after a few seconds of silence.

"What friend?" I ask intriguingly.

"Well, I guess since my party is over I guess I can go ahead and tell you now. Your friend came to the house yesterday and was choking. It looked like daddy was choking her but he said that he was helping her breath *because* she was choking."

"Wait a minute, you're saying *my* friend came to the house and she was choking and it looked like your daddy was choking her? Are you sure, Ivory-Jade? That sounds made up."

191

"No, Daddy said he was going to tell you about it after the party. He said he didn't want you to know so you wouldn't cancel my birthday party to go and see about her at the hospital."

"Nothing in the world is more important than you and celebrating your life so don't ever think that somebody else would ever come before you, okay? Can you remember her name? Can you remember what she looked like?"

"I don't know her name and she was pretty with a haircut short like Uncle Randy. I never saw her before. Her color was like you and she looked like a teenager. She looked really scared I guess because she was choking. To me it looked like daddy had his hands around her neck choking her but he told me he was just helping her so she would stop choking so I just said okay."

"I see. Did she stay long?"

"I don't think so because I don't know when she got there. After daddy helped her breathe again she left."

"This all of this happen in front of your friends?"

"No, my friends were in the back by the pool, daddy and your friend were outside of the front door. I was really, really scared when I thought daddy was choking her, but she looked okay after daddy told me to go back to my friends. Maybe you should call her and see if she's okay and maybe she can tell you were my daddy is," she confidently requests.

Why are Troy and Corbyn out to sabotage me? I have a whole lot of questions and no one is willing to give me the answers. I feel like I could literally just lose my mind right now, but some way I need to keep it together and get through tomorrow.

I think I will just keep my cell phone off for right now so I can stay focused on my goals and my event.

CHAPTER 30
A Special Concoction

TROY...

I was startled when I finally forced myself to wake up and found myself in an unknown room. I had an agonizing headache feeling like I was hit on the side of my head with a hammer or something. My ankles and wrist were bound and my mouth was taped.

The door opens and Mello appears.

"So, you finally woke up. Just nod your head to answer," he instructs. "Do you remember this room? You should, this is where you, Omar and Jamaica made movie magic.

"You're alright, you just bumped your head and knocked your dumb ass self out," Mello explains seeing the look of pain and panic on my face.

I try yelling for help but the tape just muffles my voice. I tried to free my ankles and wrists, but nothing budged to loosen the bound.

"Calm down, Troy. I ain't going to hurt you. As a matter of fact, if you relax I will take this tape off of your mouth and then I may cut you lose. It's just the two of us here so screaming won't save you. Are you going to behave?" he asks.

I nod my head yes as Mello snatches the duct tape off of my mouth. "Why am I here?" I finally was able to ask.

"Oh, you're still here at my club because we have some business to discuss. So, you never answered my question, do you remember this room?" he asks like he is show casing the scene with his hands. "This is what I like to call the *Fun Room,* where all of the fun happens, and I'm getting ready to have some real good fun with you.

"Wait, Mello, man. We can talk about all of this. We can resolve whatever is going on between us so this doesn't have to be ugly. Let's talk like real men and forget about all of this childish Honey bullshit," I plead to not be harmed.

"You know what, you're right, Mr. Troy Wilkins, let's talk. Are you okay, do you need something to eat or drink?" he calmly asks.

"Yes, I could use a little something to drink, like some water or something."

"Okay, but I know you're too good for just regular old water, so how about some cool and refreshing juice? I'm sure some cold juice would help calm some of your fears and hydrate you, huh?" he state as he walk out of the room to the bar.

Now I have to think fast, how can I get him to cut me loose?

"How am I going to drink if you have me taped up?" I asks hoping he will at least release the bounds from my wrists,

"You're right, how can you drink if I have your hands bound? I know I'm sure as hell not going to feed your ass like a bitch. Here, I'll cut the tape but you have to promise to behave."

194

A Taste Of Honey   Ravry Sloan

"I do, I promise to behave, just don't hurt me, Mello." I beg not knowing what he's going to do to me.

"So, you know I know about some of the f'cked up shit you've done over the years to other people, right?" he updates.

"Yeah, but I was just paying muthaf'cka's back for doing some dirty shit to me," I explain. "It was nothing ever personal, just business."

"Yeah, that may be true but I'm just now finding out about someone who was doing business with me that you f'cked over...bad, I mean really, really bad."

"Man, Mello, whoever it is I must not have known that they were even connected to you," I clarify guzzling down the last of my drink.

"How's your drink?   Would you like another?" he pleasantly asks.

"Yes, please."

"Now, let's see if you remember Juicy?" he asks after returning with another drink.

My heart begins to tremble remembering what I did to her.

"Juicy, yes I remember her but what in the hell does she have to do with Honey?" I ask now even more confused than ever.

For some reason I just knew all of this was about that bitch Honey, I thought, never even relating any of this to Juicy.

"Juicy was one of my top bitches. She was one of my hardest workers so when you f'cked her up, you f'cked with my money. And for that you owe me," he then reveals the root of his anger.

"I'm sorry, Mello, man! I swear I didn't know! I'll pay you for what you lost you. You will never ever hear about this shit and I will simply just walk away. I swear, Mello."

"Oh, I know we won't hear about it again, but let me to tell you why?"

Then all of a sudden my stomach began to cramp, my head began spinning and I was feeling like I had been drugged or something.

A Taste Of Honey   Ravry Sloan

"What's going on, what's happening to me?" I ask as my body begins falling limp to the floor.

"Damn, they said it would only take about five minutes, wow, they were right!"

"Five minutes for what? What's happening? Did you just drug me, again?" I ask my mouth filling with saliva.

I tried to control my gags. I did everything I could to not throw up but I soon lost the fight.

"Ding, ding, ding give this man a prize for correctly figuring out the problem! Yes, you are definitely correct, Sir. Since you f'cked up my money by drugging and f'cking up Juicy and destroying her life, I thought I'd do the same thing to you so CONGRATULATIONS, Mr. Troy Wilkins!

:And so you'll know that concoction you just wolfed down, not once but twice mind you, was a mixture of methamphetamines and crack melted to flavor up your refreshing, cool apple juice," he uncovers, laughing hysterically. "So, now, Mr. Wilkins, tell me just exactly how do you feel?"

"You muthaf'cka!" was all I can muster up to say, feeling my insides churning and my head was spinning out of control. I begin sweating and having feelings of anxiousness. "Why did you do this to me?" I ask.

"Why did you do this to Juicy? Why did you do that to Honey? I hate you type of educated nigga's with money, I swear I do! You seek out to permanently destroy people's worlds with no remorse or concern. I don't understand you muthaf'cka's!" he screams as he kicking me in my face.

I try to fight back but the drugs had my balance and timing off. I felt a few jabs but all I had the strength and discernment to do was protect my face and body from the blows and the kicks. When I couldn't fight anymore I simply gave up and collapsed back on the floor...rendered totally helpless.

"I saw the pictures of you and Jamaica f'cking and how much you liked it. I can understand that because *he* was a beautiful looking woman, but what I was especially shocked to see is how much you were really into my boy Omar. Let me repeat

196

that, *my* boy Omar! He was supposed to be the camera man only, but you seduced him.

"You looked so sexy, so strong, so hmmm," Mello states, unzipping and buckling his pants and belt.

I can see him standing there stroking his dick and licking his lips.

I close my eyes hoping this is a bad dream. I can hear him squeezing the almost empty tube of jelly, and then I heard the very familiar smacking sound. I lay there motionless hoping he is just jacking himself off, but my worst nightmare comes true.

"Just so you'll know the drugs were payback for what you did to Juicy, but this ass is what I want for payback for me. Like you said, 'this is business and not personal'," Mello repeats the statement I said earlier.

He forces my lifeless body to lay on my stomach and proceeds to pull my pants down around my ankles. He straddles over me, rubbing his dick on my ass. Aggressively pinching my butt cheeks excites him even more. He moans loudly, the nut building up within him.

"Just be still, the better I feel, the better you'll feel and the faster this will all be over with," he mumbles in an almost incoherent language.

When he couldn't take the self-inflicted tease anymore he assertively pounds his dick inside of me. He enters me over and over again, harder and harder.

I feel like I'm being ripped apart. The repetitive pain burns like fire. I eventually stop resisting causing the stinging to stop. He pumps my ass until I feel him swell. He jumps up, turns me over and forces his nut in my mouth.

He releases a roar from the sexual build up and pants as he stands over me gasping for air..

"Now I'm done with your raggedy ass! Payback is a muthaf'cking bitch!" he states, kicking me in the face.

CHAPTER 31
Web of Destruction

YODRA...HONEY... CORBYN...

This is not how I planned on this my big showing turning out at all! My mentor and lover Corbyn won't be there and I still have not heard from Troy. I called and left a voicemail telling him where we are but he never responded. Now I'm anxious, Yodra worries.

Troy and I have had our differences and arguments over the years but this is so unlike him to not communicate with me at all. It's been over two days since I last heard from him.

It's almost time for me to make my fashionably late entrance. I need to be perfect because all eyes will be on me as I walk the red carpet. I guess all alone again, until Emerson's mom brings Ivory-Jade over later to be by my side.

I have got to make the best out of this situation. Dreams can't be placed on hold because of life; because life is what makes you dream.

"I don't see her yet," states Honey observing the beautifully decorated room filled with guests.

Whispers of conversations and laughter fill the transformed gallery.

"I look a hot mess, just look at my face," expresses Honey

"I think you look fine. You look beautiful to me," Nuki compliments.

"You always know just the right thing to say, thank you. I needed to hear that," voices Honey.

"Do you think everything is okay she is not here yet?" asks Nuki looking quite confident in her debonair masculine look for the evening.

"I hope not. I think if something happened to her they would have made some type of announcement or something. They wouldn't just have us here standing around looking stupid.

"Besides, her photographs are scattered all around the room so everything should continue as planned," Honey explains while filling a glass of punch from the fountain.

"Do you think CeeCee is going to show up?" curiously inquires Nuki tossing back a glass of champagne.

"Yeah, I got the strangest feeling the shit is going down tonight. I just hope we can stop CeeCee before she finds Troy or Yodra. I'm not so confident about CeeCee's state of mind right now and what she may do," Honey expounds.

"I know when I talked to Mello earlier he said he was still with the guy and he was waiting on him to sober up so he can drop his ass off. I told you not to worry. Mello wouldn't kill him; just bust him up a little. You know, teach him a lesson." Nuki confidently states.

The guests stand around passing the time talking and enjoying the photographs on display. The live jazz band begins, drowning out the murmurs in the room.

A Taste Of Honey   Ravry Sloan

Honey admires Nuki mixing and mingling with the guest. She fit in with these uppity, snooty people like a hand in a glove. She said she was a successful business woman and she is showing her skills and working the room.

Then the announcer announces that Mrs. Yodra Wilkins was entering into the building and for the guest to prepare to greet her with a warm and excited applause.

I watch as Yodra moves smoothly down the red carpet looking stunningly beautiful and sophisticated. She stops to answer questions from reporters and to take pictures for the dozens of photographers on hand.

She is gorgeous, thought Honey. And even through all of this pomp and circumstances I can still see the hurt and emptiness in her eyes. She's getting through all of this with grace and class. But before Yodra reaches the center of the room she spots me.

"What are you doing here? I know exactly who you *really* are and the silly, little girl games you like to play! You are not welcomed here so I'm demanding that you leave now!" Yodra bullies after approaching Honey.

"Please, don't do that, Yodra. I know I am the last person you want to talk to but I have to talk to you about something," pleads Honey in Yodra's ear and hostilely grabs her arm.

"You don't have to talk to me about anything! You weren't concerned with what I thought the other night so please don't be concerned about what I think now! Can you please leave my show, now?" Yodra shouts, snatching her arm from her grasp and walking away.

Because the little confrontation was so quick the applauses never stops until Yodra made her way to the center of the venue. Yodra and her guest were given a glass of champagne for the big unison champagne toast.

"Speech, speech!" yells numerous of supporters as the champagne glasses are raised in the air.

"I'm almost never at a loss for words, but this evening I find myself somewhat speechless. I'd like to say thank you to all of you for coming out tonight and supporting my dreams. I'm not only surprised but shocked to see some of the faces that are hear.

"I've worked so hard to get to where I am and I conquered all of this by just simply stepping out on faith and fulfilling my passion. And that is to capture the world through my eyes, through my soul and through my spirit.

"I can say that this has not been a solo journey. I've had a few people praying with me, supporting me, encouraging me and mentoring me along the way. Even though I am a little embarrassed about my husbands' absence, I'd like to start off by thanking him for always supporting me..."

All of a sudden the loud noise of a door bursting open rudely interrupts Yodra's speech. A visibly drunken Corbyn stumbles in holding up the pictures of Troy in the air.

In dramatic stumbles, Corbyn bumps her way through the crowd, clapping loudly.

"The reason your husband is not by your side supporting you *again* is because that muthaf'cka is a muthaf'cking cheating bastard and I have the proof! All I've ever done is love you, Yodra and you dumped me to be back with this no good muthaf'cka!" slurs Corbyn, trying to gain her balance and composure.

The crowd gasps in shock and cautiously steps the opposite direction of Corbyn, feeling threatened.

"CeeCee, come on lets go home so I can take care of you, you're not well, Sweetheart," hints Honey easing her way closer to Corbyn and Yodra to try and maneuver Corbyn to the door.

"Get your muthaf'cking hands off of me, Honey! All of this is your fault anyway! You f'cked things up with me and my woman and you want to tell me I'm not well? You're the one with the issues!" screams Corbyn in between coughing and gagging.

Noticeably embarrassed by what Corbyn was saying, Yodra finally hollers, "What in the hell is really going on here? Corbyn, what is all of this about?"

"She's the reason all of this is going on now," Corbyn answers pointing at Honey. Then shows Yodra the photos of Troy in uncompromising positions with a young male and what looks like a transvestite.

"How does all of this make you feel, Honey?" asks Corbyn sounding condescending, spreading the photos out like a hand of playing cards.

"What do you mean how does all of this make me feel?" asks Honey sounding a slight bit aggravated.

"What is all of this?" Yodra asked looking thoroughly at the embarrassing pictures of Troy. "Do you really think you coming here like this and showing me these pictures is going to force us to get back together?" states Yodra not looking hurt anymore but pissed and humiliated.

"This is what you wanted, right? You told me you wanted to destroy Troy's world by any means necessary, well here you go! You've succeeded in his world being destroyed and all those connected. Does it feel the way you thought it would feel?" Corbyn asks Honey again, staggering to lightly slap her face.

"Could somebody please tell me what in the hell is going on?" seeks Yodra for answers.

Yodra looks confused staring back and forth between Corbyn and Honey directly in the eyes.

"What have I done to you for you to want to do this to me?" Yodra asked Honey getting closer and looking deeply in her eyes, searching for answers.

"Don't be scared now, Honey," Corbyn shouts as Honey and Nuki each grab an arm, attempting to escort her outside to try and keep the situation from escalating further.

"Awe, hell nawl, Honey, you better get your muthaf'cking hands off of me! You wanted this shit so come on now, speak up! Tell her about how you've been f'cking her husband and how he's been taking care of you, and for a couple of years now. Tell her!

"Tell her how her husband has been paying for you to live and travel and how you engage in threesomes--no, no, no, try foursomes--with her husband. Tell her!

"Tell her how you thought you were pregnant and when he found out he dumped your ass. And that all of this is your payback, your revenge for him not leaving her so he can be with you so could live happily ever after. Tell her!

"Tell her how you were going to confront her about all of this when you tricked her into taking you on a spa date. Tell her! What's the matter now, cat got your tongue now you home wrecker? Unlike you, I never wanted to wreck her home I just want to love her how she deserves to be loved," Corbyn reveals, shedding some light on the darkness of days and confusion.

Yodra stood there, obviously stunned and mortified. The room is silent with the guest feeling as uncomfortable as Yodra looks.

Tears flood Yodra's eyes; her breathing reckless and irregular and her body begins to tremble.

"How can you come here and embarrass me like this and ruin such an important day for me, you of all people?" Yodra asks slapping Corbyn's face.

"And, you, who in the hell gave you the balls to have that type of power to control somebody else's life by deciding to destroy it, Sinclair/Honey, or whatever the hell your real name is?" Yodra turns her anger towards Honey.

"You're right I do owe you some answers but this isn't the time nor the place," Honey tries to explain and wiggle out of this mess.

"Now you want to think about the right place or time, really? You and Corbyn both came here to destroy an important night for me by airing out my personal business to a room full of strangers but you can't tell me what the hell is going on?" Yodra powerfully states overflowing with emotions.

"Well, if you must know right now then here it goes. I was hurt that Troy and I broke up and that I would have to have this baby alone. I wanted your *position* and he made me feel like it would be mine one day. But, after meeting and getting to know you I just couldn't bring myself to tell you but then you presented me with an awkward opportunity of getting my revenge on Troy by showing up at y'all house. I'm sor…" was all Honey could say before she was loudly interrupted by a loud voice from the back of the room.

"Where are the f'cking violins and shit?" hollers Mello, erupting through the crowd. "Y'all bitches ain't shit! Muthaf'cka don't want yo' ass so destroying him is the answer? I swear gold digging dikes!

"How about this nigga ain't gonna be able to do a damn thing for you and nobody else now that I'm done with him," explains Mello, dragging Troy's battered body behind him.

Troy's eyes were swollen shut and blood is dripping from his nose and mouth. It was evident that he was under the control of some narcotic because he cannot stand or hold his head up.

"What's wrong with him? I thought you said you weren't going to hurt him?" asks Honey, running to Troy's side to offer aid.

"This nigga got the same shit he gave Juicy now let's see who'll respect this drugged up nigga now! This will show you that if you f'ck up my money then I'll f'ck you up for it and there it is," confidently expresses Mello, releasing the hold on Troy, forcing him to fail to the ground.

Yodra runs to Troy, pushing Honey out of the way, falling on the ground next to Troy. "Wait a minute; get your hands off of my husband! Can someone please call 9-1-1?" shrieks Yodra, concerned about Troy's well-being.

CHAPTER 32
The Love Rectangle

YODRA...HONEY...TROY...CORBYN

Troy, are you okay?" asks Yodra gently placing his head on her lap and stroking the side of his face.

"That nigga's alright.   He's embarrassed the world will know what type of man, or should I say, bitch he really is. Y'all doing all of this shit over this nigga right here, I don't get it, but y'all can have this shit. I know twelve is on the way so this is my queue to leave. Nuki, Honey, come on?" orders Mello running out the door as quickly as he came in.

Nuki, being loyal to her brother, hesitantly follows right behind him.

"I think I need to go to the hospital. I feel like my insides are on fire and I can't control my pounding, head from spinning," Troy inaudibly speaks, barely holding his head up.

"Okay, Baby, 9-1-1 has already been called. Where have you been? I've been so worried. Wasn't that the guy who brought you home the other night when you thought you had been drugged?" Yodra asks feeling confused.

"Please forgive me, Baby?" Troy sluggishly begs Yodra.

"Mama, Mama, congratulations on your picture show!" Ivory-Jade excitedly screams, running up to them energized about the night.

"Hey, Daddy! What happened to my daddy?" she asks with the smile disappearing from her face. She sees Troy and Yodra on the floor and observes Troy's bleeding face.

"No, Barbara, please take her back! Please!" Yodra appeals with Emerson's mother. Before Barbara was able to get Ivory-Jade's hand and take her away Corbyn grabs her, picks her up and wraps her arms tightly around her.

"CeeCee, what are you doing? You don't want to hurt her daughter," pleas Honey. "I know you're going through some things right now but I know you don't want to hurt an innocent child, do you? This isn't going to fix or change a thing."

"Corbyn, please put my daughter down," begs Yodra slowly easing her way towards where they were standing.

Corbyn begins rocking her body from side to side; noticeably squeezing Ivory-Jade's little body in her arms.

"All I ever wanted to do was love you," Corbyn responds sobbing. "I thought you loved me, too? I thought you wanted somebody to love you and treat you right but I guess that shit was a joke! You dumped me for this nigga."

"Corbyn, I'm sorry that you're hurting right now, and we can most definitely talk about it, but harming my daughter will not be the answer to solving our problems either. Please, Corbyn, if you ever loved me the way you say you do please let Ivory-Jade go, please?" Yodra begs again for her daughter to be released.

A Taste Of Honey   Ravry Sloan

"I'm sorry, too, for everything that I have ever done to hurt you as well," Honey chimes in with an apology. "I saw your secret room, CeeCee, and I think it's time that we take you to get the help that you need to cope with life and reality right now."

"Help, I don't need no damn help, I got this! Now get out of my damn face!" Corbyn replies pushing Honey to the side.

"So now you want to talk, Yodra? Hmmp, I've been trying to talk to you for the past couple of days and you didn't have the human consideration to return not one of my phone calls. Or respond to any of my text messages but now you want to talk?" Corbyn declares bursting in a boisterous laugh.

Ivory-Jade starts showing the first signs of fear about everything that was going on and began to cry. "I want my daddy, I want my daddy!" she screams and began kicking and trying to wiggle her way out of Corbyn's arms.

"So tell me something new little girl! It seems like everybody wants your damn daddy but nobody seems to want me. What in the hell is wrong with me?"

"Between Honey's gold-digging, horny, ass and your mama's unhappy, confused, curious ass I can't seem to think straight. I feel like, I'm losing a grip on reality or something

"I was always taught if I treat people how I want to be treated then I will be treated back the same...BULLSHIT! All I do is love and love hard but that's just never good enough for some people," she alleges, as Ivory-Jade begins fidgeting.

"Daddy! Daddy, help me!" Ivory-Jade squealing for her Daddy's help, again!

"Corbyn, no, please put Ivory-Jade down so we can go outside and talk. You're hurting her!" Yodra screams, trying to pry Ivory-Jade out of her arms. "I promise we can work something out, please, please, Corbyn, please give Ivory-Jade to me."

"Get back, Yodra!" Corbyn cries when seemingly from thin air she pulls out one of the platinum, scalpel sharp spatulas from the custom artist took kit I gave her as a gift.

"I love you so much and I thought you loved me back! Why, Yodra, why? This nigga treats you like a piece of trash but

209

you can't seem to leave him. Other than a dick what else can this muthaf'cka do that I haven't done?" Corbyn says while easing the grip from around Ivory-Jade's body loose a bit and now pointing the sharp spatula at Troy.

"What's happening?" Troy asks trying to gain composure by standing up and appearing to sober up. "Give me my daughter!"

"Sit your ass back down, Troy Wilkins! I got this shit right now. You had your turn and you messed all of that up with the both of them," Corbyn demands letting one of her arms go from around Ivory-Jade to wildly wave the spatula in the air.

"Okay, Corbyn, I was wrong and I apologize from the bottom of my heart, but after you give me my daughter, we can sit down and talk about this more in depth. I promise," Yodra calmly pleads for Corbyn to settle down while still holding Ivory-Jade.

"I hate you so much right now I could just kill you, but that would not get rid of my problem," Corbyn responds focusing her attention back to Troy. "What will make me really feel better is if I would just eliminate the problems that are keeping me and you from being together and that problem is you, Mr. Troy Wilkins,"

"What? You may be *pretending* you're a man but I am the one with balls. You can't be mad that you don't have what it takes to satisfy and keep a woman. I know I'm a man, make no excuses about that, but the funny thing is I don't think you realize that you're not!

"I may be drugged right now but I would never sit back and let you hurt my daughter so don't even think about it," Troy bellows through the pain, desperately trying to hold himself up. "Give me my muthaf'cking daughter now!" Troy demands.

Corbyn dives at Troy with the spatula, missing him and causing her to stumble a little.

"Corbyn…CeeCee, please let Ivory-Jade go, please?" pleads Yodra and Honey in harmony as the rest of the guest inhale in shock.

Just then the police barges through the door in a loud chaos of loud orders and guns drawn. "Put the little girl and the knife down, Ma'am, so nobody will be hurt!" orders the officer.

"No! No! No! No!" Corbyn shrills wrapping both of her arms back around Ivory-Jade, still holding the spatula. "Nobody loves me anyway so why should I care about you shooting me? Who will mourn for me?"

"Ma'am, will you at least put the child down so we can talk about getting you some help," the officer states walking slowly towards Corbyn. "I think you may be scaring the little girl. Come on, Ma'am, you don't want to hurt her; do you?"

"CeeCee, I will mourn for you if something happens to you. But that's not going to happen, right? I'm so sorry for hurting you, I truly am, and I know you may not believe this but I do still love you, CeeCee," begs Honey. "Come on, let Ivory-Jade go and do what's right."

The more and more Honey talks, the less focus Corbyn has with grip on Ivory-Jade. Yodra benefits from the distraction by leaning in to take hold of Ivory-Jade.

Troy sees what Yodra is doing and in sync, the two charge in the direction of Corbyn with efforts to seize Ivory-Jade from her clutch. There was a scuffle between Troy, Yodra and Corbyn, Ivory-Jade caught in the middle. Among all of the commotion, Yodra was able to get Ivory-Jade freed from Corbyn's grip.

"No! This is not how it is supposed to end," shouts Corbyn with the look of fear and uncertainty all over her face, still holding the now bloody spatula.

"Drop the knife, Ma'am!" barks the officer again.

Troy fell to the ground moaning and holding his chest while the blood oozed through his fingers.

"Troy!" screams Yodra, she and Ivory-Jade fall to the floor beside him to comfort him.

"Yodra, I never meant to hurt you in any way so let me apologize from the bottom of my heart if I did," Corbyn reveals, holding the bloody spatula to her wrist and looking as if she is just ready to give up.

"And I want to say this last thing to you, I may not have been able to fulfill your dreams but I know I was never your nightmare. Just remember that you certainly deserve better than

211

Troy and how he treats you. Please just try to always remember all I ever did was love you…I LOVE YOU, YODRA WILKINS," she declares.

In the blink of an eye she slit her wrist as her lifeless body falls to the floor. There were screams and breaths of disbelief from the on-lookers as the police charge to assess the body. A silence fell upon the room with the blaring sounds of the sirens in the background.

Honey slowly crawls to Corbyn's body and kisss her lightly on the lips. "Why? Why did she have to do something so dumb like this!" she squawks in a whaling, uncontrollable cry. "I'll always love you, CeeCee, always and forever."

1 YEAR LATER...

CORBYN...

Corbyn actually survives the attempted suicide with the sharp artist spatula. After being taken to the hospital for treatment and evaluation, she was committed to a mental facility to deal with her delusional thoughts and behaviors. No one knew about the mental disorders Corbyn faced daily as she tried to channel it through her photography. The heart-ache and heart-breaks she experienced sent her in a tail spin of confusion, betrayal and hurt...causing her to lose a grip of reality.

HONEY...

Honey had a healthy baby boy that ironically she named, Croy, after Corbyn and Troy. Unfortunately, Honey was convicted for five years for conspiracy of kidnapping and black mail against Troy. The courts award fulltime, custody to the biological father

213

and his family to continue raising Croy while Honey serves out the remainder of her prison sentence.

NUKITA...

Nukita was also charged with conspiracy of kidnapping and black mail and is also serving a five year prison sentence. She and Honey have continued to stay in communication and are planning on being in a relationship with her once they are released.

MELLOW...

Mellow was charged with kidnapping, black mail, rape (sodomy) and attempted murder and is serving a 12 year prison sentence.

TROY...

Troy recovers from his rape and drug ingested overdose. He spent a couple of weeks in a rehabilitation center trying to build a resistance to his new found weakness. Troy apologizes to Yodra for all of the distrust he has created within their marriage and wants desperately for things to work out.

YODRA...

Yodra and Troy sought marriage counseling after Troy's release from the rehabilitation center. They are faithfully committed to working on the issues that have invaded their marriage and caused this deep discourse between them. Yodra's photography career is very successful and with a lot of help and hard-work, she is finally excited to be dedicated to rebuilding her marriage!

And last but not least...little baby boy Croy is adjusting and becoming an accepted member of The Wilkins' family, along with Troy's other son Joshua, which he fathered with Juicy. Troy and Yodra have permanent custody of Joshua because they decided they could afford better medical care for him and provide a better life for him in the long term. After finding out the truth about Troy drugging Juicy, Yodra wouldn't accept anything less than making sure the right steps are taken to rectify his wrongs.

Book Discussion Questions:

1) Do you think trying to repair the issues in a marriage or relationship can be fixed outside of the home?

2) Do you think as a wife or girlfriend you have the right to address the mistress about the man?

3) How would you handle your significant other having an extra marital affair?

4) If you had concerns in reference to your relationship, would you address them with your significant other? Or do you express them with someone else to get sympathy, revenge or to simply have an empty void filled?

5) Have you ever thought about participating in a ménage à trois?

6) Have you ever been curious or had thoughts about being with someone intimately of the same sex?

7) What is the most risqué thing you would do to keep your relationship happy?

8) Would you be someone's secret lover?

9) Would you raise a child conceived from an extra marital affair?

10) How would you feel if you found out your significant other had an affair with someone of the same sex?